THE UNFORGIVING DAUGHTER

* * * * * *

MANUELA SCHNEIDER

WOLFPACK PUBLISHING
— EST 2013 —

Paperback Edition

Copyright © 2021 (As Revised) Manuela Schneider

Wolfpack Publishing
6032 Wheat Penny Avenue
Las Vegas, NV 89122

wolfpackpublishing.com

Paperback ISBN 978-1-64734-268-5
eBook ISBN 978-1-64734-267-8

THE UNFORGIVING DAUGHTER

******

ACKNOWLEDGEMENTS

***

I WANT TO THANK THE FOLLOWING PEOPLE FOR MAKING THIS BOOK POSSIBLE:

My wonderful editor Denise F. Mc Allister. Not only has she done a wonderful job editing my books but also blessed me with great advice and expertise. I have learned tons about writing since working with her.

My publicist Krista Rolfzen Soukup of Blue Cottage agency who has designed a new path of following my dream for me.

Bestselling author Harlan Hague, who has helped me tremendously on my way. He never got tired of answering my numerous emails and connected me with inspiring people to work with.

Pam Van Allen who has done a great job with proof-reading the entire story.

Award winning author Rod Timanus for keeping my spirit high for writing.

***

I DEDICATE THIS BOOK TO ALL THE LAWMEN OF THE SOUTHWEST FRONTIER DAYS who battled cattle rustlers, murderers, thieves, and political power struggles. Even lawmen were tempted to switch sides from time to time, but who are we to judge them? Times were harsh, the law of the six-shooter was stronger than the written word in the law books and only the strongest survived. But in the end, justice always wins.

CHAPTER ONE

***

IT WAS A SUNNY MORNING IN YUMA, ARIZONA AND PEOPLE ENJOYED THE CRISP air after the searing summer months in the Territory. The cooler weather was a relief.

Eleonora hummed a song while she washed some of her father's shirts with her late mother's washboard. Everyone in town liked the sheriff's daughter and fondly called her Elli. With dark hair like the wing of a raven, just like her father's, she was the spitting image of her beautiful red-haired Irish mother. Humble and charming, she was also a tough young lady.

Oscar Townsend was a well-respected man in town. He represented the law, not only in Yuma but also in the nearby mining town of Castle Dome.

Townsfolk joined him in mourning the loss of his wife, and did their best to watch over his only child, Eleonora. Now Elli was all grown up and helped her father wherever she could.

She knew her Pa loved her dearly, yet she had always been aware that he wished to also have a son. Elli tried her best to be the son Oscar would most likely never have. So far, he hadn't remarried. Too deep was the pain of having lost his beloved wife.

Although Elli was an outstanding beauty, she never bragged about it. She didn't mind getting her hands dirty, could ride better than most men, and possessed outstanding marksmanship. Her father often teased that he would have to hire her as his deputy if she continued to develop her skills. That always made her smile. As she grew up, she became aware of the increasing danger in the Western frontier, especially when greed for land, gold, and silver took over a man's heart. Elli learned to always be on alert in order to protect herself as well as her father.

One day Sheriff Townsend brought in an outlaw he had arrested close to the California border. The posse had been on the hunt for the man after a marshal from the California Territory had asked for help. Elli was sure glad to see her father return safely.

The man who sat on an extra horse was said to have murdered his wife and parents-in-law. *What a monster he must be*, Elli thought.

As she walked closer to the group, she waved at her father who got off his horse. He looked worn out and dusty, and for the first time Elli was aware of a few strands of gray hair around his temples. Sheriff Townsend walked the prisoner into the jail. Elli was surprised to see a very handsome man with a friendly face and dark features. He didn't look at all as she had expected a murderer to look. In fact, she was stunned when he bowed his head and gave her a friendly greeting. He behaved like a gentleman of the first water, a diamond in the dust. His voice was husky and had a soothing tone. Quickly Elli turned away from him and followed her father into the sheriff's office.

"Oh, Pa, I'm so glad you've returned home safely."

"I'm mighty glad, too, Princess! Sure missed your cooking on the trail."

"Tell me, that longrider you arrested, did he really kill his wife and her parents as the people outside are saying?"

Her father paused, then said, "I don't know Elli, I really don't know. Somehow, he seems like a nice guy. Didn't cause any commotion when we arrested him. He's the son of a Spanish noble family.

"Nevertheless, the evidence speaks against him; at least if you believe the judge in Orange Grove. Well, I guess that's something they'll have to decide in their trial when they get him back to California. I just packed the parcel for them."

The next day Elli brought over some homemade food to her father's office since he had some work to catch up on after being gone for days. She also packed a portion for the prisoner in the pokey as she didn't believe in bread and water punishment. Her Pa had taught her to be careful, but also to believe in the innocence of people until proven guilty.

As Elli walked over to the cell, the man behind the bars jumped up from his simple bunk bed. He was almost two heads taller than her, and his shoulders were broad. Black, shoulder-length, wavy hair. Eyes dark like a strong cup of cowboy coffee. Elli couldn't deny that he appeared handsome despite his unshaved look.

"I thank you for the food, ma'am. This is very kind of you. May God bless you, Miss."

"You dare to talk of God's blessing after being arrested for murder?" It hadn't been her intention to be rude, but for the first time she felt insecure in the presence of a man, and it confused her.

Elli saw the hurt her words had caused. His eyes became

a shade darker, and he turned away without saying another word. Walking toward the door, Elli mumbled an apology.

The prisoner addressed her. "Miss Townsend, you have been kind enough to bring me this meal so I will give you some advice. On the trail fleeing from the people in my hometown, I met some road agents—"banditos" as we would say. They spoke about a town called Castle Dome and a sheriff named Oscar Townsend. I believe they plan an ambush, and I am certain your father is in grave danger."

Elli turned pale. When she asked for details, he shook his head. "That is all I heard. Despite my reputation, I do not spend my days in the company of ruthless criminals. Just watch out and tell him to be prepared. Thank you once again for the food, Miss Townsend."

She nodded, looked him straight in the eye. "Eleonora, my name is Eleonora, and I will remember your words, Mister--"

"Armando. Armando Phillipe Diaz."

Elli left the jail, deep in thought, not even paying attention to the townsfolk who greeted her. The warning sounded genuine. She knew her father had a dangerous job, but this sounded more like a plot against him.

Maybe those outlaws were intent on robbing the mining community? Elli decided to tell her father and to caution him to watch out for any strangers coming into town.

About a week later a posse from Orange Grove arrived in Yuma. After a decent meal and a good night's rest for the posse members, they escorted the prisoner back to California to face trial there. The men treated him harshly; they obviously believed him to be guilty of murdering three people. When he walked by Elli he nodded and whispered, "Do not forget what I told you. May God protect you, Eleonora!"

She nodded, believing his warning to be sincere. As the group rode out of town, Elli remained on the steps of the Sheriff's office long after the dusty cloud from the horses had settled, watching. The loving daughter told her father about the warning, and it left him thoughtful, too, but right now there was nothing he could do about it. They had increased the size of the jail twice already; it seemed that ruthless behavior and law breaking were on the rise in the Yuma area. The "crowbar hotel," as the locals called the county jail, was often full."

A few days later, the warning almost forgotten, the mining community of Castle Dome instructed Sheriff Townsend to escort the monthly transport of gold from the mine.

Although Castle Dome was mainly known for its lead ore, prospecting gold and silver was also a successful endeavor. However, the bank was in Yuma and renegade Apaches were a problem in the area.

The wagon carried its precious load, including a hired shotgun on top and the sheriff and deputy as escort. It was about twenty miles to Yuma and the country was flat except for a few outcrops of big boulders. As the group passed the rocks, gunfire exploded around them, sending the driver and the gunman on top of the coach plunging to the ground. Oscar Townsend pulled his gun and jerked his horse around to find shelter behind the wagon, when his deputy took lead a few feet from him.

Sheriff Townsend felt a stinging pain under his right shoulder blade and knew he'd been hit. The impact caused him to lose his balance and slide from the saddle. His boot caught in the stirrup, and his terrified horse sprinted away from the gunfire in the direction of Yuma, dragging his rider. Townsend knew it was the end for him.

With tears in his eyes, he thought of his beloved daughter, Elli. He imagined her lovely face, so much like her mother's features, as the horse dragged him over rocks and dust, tumbleweeds and cactus. Her angelic image was the last thing in the sheriff's mind before his life ended.

When the horse galloped into the main street of Yuma, the panicked animal still dragged the bleeding body of the dead lawman. Men quickly jumped into its path and calmed the lathered horse, holding him steady so they could carefully remove the boot from the stirrup and lead the horse away. People stood in shock around their fallen sheriff as Elli came running down the street. With an almost inhuman sounding scream, she sank to the ground of the dusty street, cradling her cherished father and weeping inconsolably.

The funeral took place two days later. Elli stood at the fresh grave next to her mother's. All alone! An orphan now in a world where the influenza had taken her Mom, and devilish, greedy men had murdered her Pa. She had no more tears left. Instead, an unfamiliar emotion formed in her chest like a burning flame. It was raging, consuming hatred, vengeance to get even with the men who had robbed her beloved father's life. She clutched his sheriff's badge so tightly in her right hand that the pin pierced her flesh. Blood stained the tin badge, sealing her oath to take revenge, and force those outlaws to face the justice they deserved. *Yes, they'll pay for what they've done.*

CHAPTER TWO

***

ELLI SAT IN THEIR HOUSE, THE HOUSE THAT BELONGED TO HER ALONE NOW. SO full of memories of her parents that she could hardly bear to stay. But where would she start? How could she ever find the men who had killed her father?

She didn't even know what they looked like. No, *she* didn't, but one man did, the handsome Spaniard who most likely had been hanged by now. He had seen the killers.

Elli had no time to lose. She had to find out if the man was still awaiting his trial. In case he was alive, he might be able to describe the "banditos," as he had called them. Quickly packing two saddlebags with food and spare clothes, she changed into riding pants and a shirt belonging to father. Burying her face in it, she was consumed with grief. Donning his shirt and smelling his masculine scent, almost felt as if he were embracing her, yet she knew he would never hug her again for the rest of her life. Swallowing tears, Elli walked over to the barn to saddle her own horse, a strong stallion named Thunder.

Before mounting, she holstered her father's gun and slid his shotgun into the scabbard on the saddle.

His sheriff's badge was pinned inside her vest as a steady reminder of her mission and with whom she was dealing. Eleonora Townsend rode off into the late morning. No one stopped or questioned her about where she was headed. The hunt for her father's murderers had begun.

* * *

Elli was not a spoiled woman, and she didn't mind sleeping at a campfire with nothing but some jerky and dry bread in her stomach. She tried hard not to give into the desperate feeling of loneliness, and often prayed and thought about her father. Determined to ride to Orange Grove for information as to whether Armando Diaz had been hanged already, she hoped she was not too late. Thinking about Armando, she had to admit he had impressed her. So far, her father had been the only man ever to achieve that. Elli missed him terribly and hoped she could take revenge in his name.

She slept little; her pistol close at her side. Every animal sound played tricks in her mind. Up before dawn, the Sheriff's daughter continued her challenging ride against time.

Finally, five days after her father's funeral, she arrived in Orange Grove, surrounded by orange groves. It was easy to see how the town got its name as well as some obvious wealth, judging by the stately buildings. The smell of the orange trees was so refreshing compared to the dusty air in Yuma. Elli knew that noble families from Spain had started this settlement. Her father had told her that Armando was a member of such a prominent family. What could have caused him to murder people if he had riches? But she didn't know if he was really guilty, or did she? According to the telegram asking for her Dad's help, the man had shot his wife and in-laws with a double barrel shotgun and run away, which of course proved his guilt, or so the judge said.

However, the whole story didn't seem to sound right. Elli had developed a gut feeling about criminals after watching her father handle them for many years. Armando just didn't fit the characteristics of a cold-blooded murderer.

As she rode into town, she mumbled to herself, "Well, this looks rather lush compared to the desert of the Arizona Territory." Her horse nickered as if in agreement. Despite the serious situation, she chuckled and patted the stallion's neck. He was a good companion.

Elli was aware that the townsfolk watched and whispered behind their hands. They all wore fine garments, and she looked out of place with her dusty men's clothing and the pistol holster dangling from her hip. But she didn't care and asked directions to the sheriff's office. Once there, the tired woman climbed down from the saddle.

It had been a tough ride, and she felt every hour of it in her dragged-out body. As she entered the office, a man in his early thirties stood up to greet her. He wore a shark's smile. "Howdy Miss, what can I do for you?" For some reason, Elli disliked him right from the start.

"I'm Sheriff Townsend's daughter. I need to talk to your lag, Armando Philippe Diaz, the man that my father arrested for you." Elli hadn't missed the change in the man's expression. He seemed uncomfortable and not as self-secure as he had been when she first walked in.

"Why would you want to talk to him, and why didn't your father come himself if he has business to settle with the man?"

Elli's gut feeling told her to keep the truth to herself. Instead of spilling the beans she smiled and shrugged her shoulders. "He's busy rounding up cattle rustlers, and I was curious to see your beautiful town anyway."

His beaming smile made it obvious that the man was

flattered by the charming young woman. "My name is Harris, Steven Harris. I'm sorry I have to disappoint you, but you can't talk to Diaz."

"You probably hanged him already, haven't you?"

"Wished we had, but the son-of-a-gun escaped. No idea how he achieved it, but we're on the hunt for him. He won't escape justice, that's for sure."

"I might hang around in town for a day or two. Let me know in case you find out something, please. I'll stay across the street at the Casa Grande Hotel."

"I certainly will, ma'am. But you haven't told me yet what you need to know from that murderer. Maybe I could help you," he added with a greedy appraisal of her body. Elli shook her head.

"We were just wondering if he had met folks my father and husband are searching for." She was aware of his in-appropriate looks and quickly added the lie about having a husband. She didn't want to have Harris trailing her.

After Elli rented a room at the hotel, she sat on her bed, devastated on the one hand because no one knew where Armando was, relieved on the other that he was still alive. Where could she search for him? The desperate woman had to find him before the posse did because they would probably hang him without trial just to make sure he didn't escape again.

CHAPTER THREE

✱✱✱

"WELL, IT DOESN'T MAKE SENSE TO TRY TO THINK ON AN EMPTY STOMACH," she mumbled to herself. She washed her face at the ceramic bowl and walked down the street to the restaurant she had seen when she first rode into town. As Elli stepped into the place, she was surprised at how nice it was. Glass pitchers of fresh water and homemade lemonade sat on some tables. The restaurant looked clean and quite busy. The meal of the day was meatloaf with mashed potatoes and gravy, and while she waited for her food, the mouthwatering aromas made her stomach growl like a hungry wolf.

The lady, who was obviously the owner of the "Lucky Pot," was friendly, and she quickly brought a plate with a delicious-smelling meal. Elli marveled at the food.

The restaurant owner smiled. "Like it?"

"Oh yes, it tastes delicious, just the way my late mom used to prepare meatloaf."

"Then you should also have a piece of my homemade apple cake and a cup of coffee to go with it, my dear. By the way, what brings you to town? Are you with the cattle drive folks?" She asked with a side glance to Elli's dusty clothes.

Elli answered the question with hearty laughter. "No, I actually had to talk to the sheriff and maybe will have to talk to the judge today as well. I'm here on behalf of my father and need to get some information about a suspect he arrested, a man named Armando Philippe Diaz."

The restaurant owner turned pale. "May I sit with you for a minute?"

"Of course. After all, it is your restaurant, isn't it?" Elli was curious to hear what the lady had to say.

"Armando has fled. Nobody knows where he is. His wife and her family were well known and liked among the townsfolk. Nobody knows what triggered that tragedy. To be honest, I've known Armando since he was a child when his parents came over from the Old World to start their big estancia.

"I never believed, and never will, that he murdered his family. He dearly loved his wife Maria, and respected her parents. If you ask me, this whole case is a crazy witch hunt, but it is a fact that Maria and her parents were found dead. The last time Armando was seen, he was close to the mountains that border his ranch. I know that men have to obey the law, but if that posse reporting to that corrupt judge lays hands on him, I guarantee you it will end in a lynch party.

"The poor feller knows it too and most likely he's trying to find out more about the killings by himself. By the way, forgive me for being so rude, I am Ruby Hershberger, the owner and cook of the Lucky Pot restaurant."

"Elli, Elli Townsend. I need Mister Diaz's help and really have to find him on an urgent matter. I wish I knew where he was."

The elder lady seemed to recognize the despair in the young woman's voice and remained silent for a moment.

Then she looked up at her. "I have always loved that boy. He has grown into a fine young gentleman. I can't bring myself to see him as a murderer. I know Armando has spent a lot of time in those mountains bordering his ranch. Even calls them his place of serenity when he needs to think. I imagine the guy might hide there."

"Thank you so much for that information. By the way, why did you call your judge corrupt?"

Ruby looked around, then bowed her head and whispered, "He never liked Armando, always wanted that ranch, but the Diaz family wouldn't sell it. That didn't set well with the judge, if you understand what I mean." Elli nodded thoughtfully.

"I'll get your cake and coffee now, on the house. I hope you find him before they do," Ruby pointed outside as the sheriff and a well-clad gentleman walked by. "Judge Werdinger, that is." She got up to fetch the dessert.

Elli returned to the hotel after her meal and decided to get some rest to prepare for the search the following day. The more she thought about the whole case, the more confusing it seemed.

Something simply wasn't right and the young woman was determined to find the truth. She needed Armando's help if she ever wanted to find her father's murderers.

At dawn Elli headed over to the "Lucky Mule Livery" and checked on her horse. He was an impressive stallion, black as a moonless night, strong and muscular. She had paid the stable boy extra to take good care of him, making sure he was well fed, watered, and brushed down.

Elli walked over to the restaurant and ask Ruby to prepare some provisions for her trip. Ruby was only too happy to help out and while preparing cold cut meat and biscuits, also quickly made a plate of scrambled eggs with bacon and beans. The lady had taken an immediate liking to the girl and was hoping she might be able to help Armando.

As she was eating, Elli overheard the conversation of two ranchers at a nearby table. Elli turned to watch from the corner of her eye. "What will happen to the ranch now? Do you think the judge will lay his hands on it?"

The second rancher answered firmly. "Not as long as Armando is alive. He'll never agree to that."

"Don't be a fool. As soon as they find him, they'll hang him from the next tree. They won't even bother to bring him into town for trial."

"Well, that's probably true. I'm sure Judge Werdinger won't waste any time. He was after that estate for as long as I can remember. I just don't get what in the world got into Armando to put the kibosh on his own folks."

"Hell, we don't even know if he did it. He was always like a true Thoroughbred to do business with and everybody knows he loved that woman with all his heart."

The other man nodded in agreement, pulled out a few dollars, and pushed back his chair. "Well, work is waiting for me. See you Sunday at church, partner." Elli's gaze followed them more carefully than ever.

"Did you enjoy the breakfast, dear? By the way, here's your lunch parcel. God be with you, girl."

Elli thanked the friendly woman and promised she would try her best.

There was no other choice because Elli believed neither she nor her father would find peace if she failed. "Ruby, one more question. Why in the world is the judge so determined to get Armando's ranch?"

Ruby carefully looked around, scanning the crowd in the restaurant. "Well, the judge doesn't care for the ranch itself. It's the piece of land he's after. Nobody really knows his true motive. But when Werdinger has some idea in his head, he'll pursue it at any cost."

After saddling her horse, Elli packed her pistol and her rifle and rode out of town. As soon as Orange Grove was left behind, she urged Thunder into a faster canter toward the mountains where Armando Phillipe Diaz most likely was hiding.

At first, Elli couldn't find any traceable tracks. *The townspeople and posse must have trampled all over the place like a herd of buffaloes.*

She tried to put herself in Armando's shoes. What would she do on the run? He definitely needed shelter for the night so either an abandoned cabin or a cave would most likely be the kind of place where he would hide.

CHAPTER FOUR

***

SHE RODE TOWARD THE MOUNTAINS THAT BORDERED ARMANDO'S RANCH, following the description Ruby had given her for where to start looking. This clue helped to eliminate the endless possibilities for where he could be hiding in the rugged terrain.

Armando must have mentioned a cave to Ruby some years back, in the Cougar Canyon. According to Ruby, the canyon got its name from a cougar-shaped shadow that only appeared on the east wall around noon time.

It was past noon already. But as Elli was beginning to think she'd never get to the place ... and Thunder rounded the bend, the cougar-shaped shadow appeared on one of the canyon walls.

"Dang, it's about time, thought I'd never find it," she mumbled. She was racing against time, and the threat of a lynch mob posse bore down on her.

Approaching the canyon wall, she got off her horse to lead him because Elli didn't want the precious animal to hurt himself on the jagged rocks. Looking up, she finally saw the entrance of a small cave that hadn't been visible from the bottom of the canyon.

"Well, I would say that's a mighty fine place to hide. What do you think, Thunder?" The horse nickered in agreement, and she patted him gently on his neck. The magnificent stallion was the only link left to her father besides the house and sheriff's badge in her vest pocket. The woman loved the beautiful horse dearly.

Elli's instinct told her that Armando was up there. She also knew she made an easy target in the open terrain and avoided making noise of any kind. The climb up to the cave was strenuous and after a few minutes she was short of breath, but finally caught the faint smell of a campfire.

Certain that by now Armando must be aware that someone was getting much too close to his hiding place, if he was there, Elli decided to announce herself rather than taking the risk of running into a bullet.

She called out his name carefully. "Armando Diaz, are you in there? It's Elli Townsend from Yuma. Please, Armando, I really need to talk to you. It's about my father."

At first there was no answer and Elli thought she must have been mistaken to think he was in this small cave. But as she was about to leave, a voice whispered back at her. "Did anybody follow you? Where is the damn posse?" Spinning around, the rocks under her boots slid and she almost lost her balance.

Armando stood in the shady entrance of the cave aiming a rifle at her. She swallowed hard. He looked terrible—exhausted, and hollow-eyed. His right temple showed traces of dried blood from an ugly gash, and his face was bruised. Obviously, he had taken a lacing after the posse members picked him up in Yuma. She felt sorry for him. He looked at her and his face changed.

"Eleonora, what are you doing here in California? Why

did you come looking for me? Has something happened to your father?" She was unable to speak, simply confirmed his suspicion with a nod and tears in her eyes.

"Come into the cave and tell me what happened. I'm sorry I can't offer you a more comfortable accommodation but, as you surely know by now, I had to flee from that lynch mob posse."

"Why did you run away? That makes you look guiltier than ever."

"Do you really think I would get a fair trial? Have you met the townsfolk yet? You must have met Ruby. She is the only person in town I ever told about this cave. If I want to prove that I'm innocent, I have to find the true murderer. I can't do that if they hang me, now can I?"

She stared at him. He laughed, but it was a bitter sound.

"You probably believe them that I killed my wife and her parents. But I tell you, I did not."

"Why don't you tell me your side of the story then?"

He stared into the embers of the campfire, carefully poking at it and trying not to raise any smoke. Elli got up, walked over to Thunder, and unpacked her saddlebag. Returning to the fire, she handed Armando some of the food Ruby had prepared. His eyes grew huge; it was apparent he hadn't eaten much in days. The handsome Spaniard took her hand gently and she blushed, not prepared for the tender touch of his rough hands.

"This is the second time you are feeding me. I hope God grants me the chance to spoil you with a huge meal someday, Elli Townsend."

She smiled, and took a bite of her bread, waiting in silence until he was ready to tell his side of the story.

"Maria was the love of my life." His voice was barely above a whisper. She waited for him to continue. "We were happy and, unlike most marriages among Spanish noblemen, ours was not an arranged marriage. I would never have harmed her.

"We were caught in the middle of a dirty and corrupt game. I faced threats because I wasn't willing to sell my ranch to the greedy man who builds the railway in California. My land is right in the center of where his railway is planned. It would save those people lots of time to own my land, plus the property around the tracks will be of tremendous worth someday soon.

"I was searching for a few horses that had escaped our corral the previous night. When I returned, I could not find my wife at first. I thought she would be in the kitchen cooking for me. Oh, God, she was a fantastic cook!"

His voice trailed off, seemingly lost in painful memories. Elli remained silent. When he spoke again, she saw a single tear rolling down his cheek. Armando didn't try to hide his tears.

"Finally, I walked into our bedroom to change my shirt, and there she was, lying on our bed, staring at the ceiling. Around her was a terrible pool of blood, and the room smelled like iron. She was still breathing, but shallow. I tried to stop the bleeding from a huge gunshot wound in her stomach. She was so pale, Elli. She whispered something, but it was difficult to hear her. I didn't know what to do."

"What did she say?" Elli wanted to know.

He shook his head. "It was barely understandable; all I could make out was the word 'railway.' "

"She smiled at me, although I could tell she was in so much pain; then she simply stopped breathing. Maria died in my arms and there wasn't anything I could do about it!"

She could feel his anger and grief. His hand clenched into a fist and he shivered. Elli knew the pain raging through his chest all too well from seeing her father's body.

"Where were your parents-in-law?" He stared blankly as if he had to remind himself to return back to the present day in the cave. How lost and devastated he looked. Elli had to fight the urge to hug him.

"I called out for them, but there was no answer. When I walked over to the barn, I found them. My father-in-law was shot, and lying behind the barn door. My mother-in-law was next to the saddles; they had shot her in the head. I remember she was still holding a hayfork to protect herself.

"A danged hayfork! There was so much blood every-where. I panicked and ran away because I knew as the only survivor, most likely I would become the main suspect. If I wanted to find the real cutthroats and punish them, I had to be free. So, I fled and tried to hide across the border in your territory until I would be able to sneak back into California and hunt down those who did this to my family. This is when your father put me in shackles.

"It is too dangerous for them to keep me alive, you understand? They try to put the blame on me. That way they can steal my ranch and get rid of the only witness who truly knows that they bushwhacked my entire family."

"Who are they, Armando?" He looked out of the cave for a few moments. When he turned his face toward her, she was shocked to see blind hatred burning on his face.

"It had to have been the judge and his corrupt rail-way-building brother. I must get revenge for Maria and her parents. It is a matter of justice, do you understand that, Elli?"

Of course, she understood. After all, she was in the same situation, wasn't she?

For the first time he studied her pale complexion and the dark circles under her eyes.

"What happened, Elli, why are you here?"

The desperate woman swallowed hard, fighting back her own tears. "It happened exactly as you said. They robbed the mine's monthly gold load. The cowards ambushed everybody escorting it, including my father." She was blind with tears now, and Armando put an arm around her shoulders. She sobbed but tried hard to control herself.

"You are the only one who knows what those road agents look like. I need to find them. I must see them pay for what they did even if that means killing them. For the sake of my father and in the name of justice. I may go to hell for it, but it doesn't matter. I won't leave until I take revenge for my Pa who always had been a man of the law."

Armando stared at her. "Isn't it an amazing thing with God's mysterious ways? There, he sends you into my life ... How tragically our destinies are connected. I am so sorry about your father's fate. I have never hated so much that what I predicted came true a few weeks ago. And I admire your grit to ride out here determined to find me. But I also have to admit that I don't know if I can help you. For sakes alive, I don't even know if I will survive this mess."

CHAPTER FIVE

***

FOR THE FIRST TIME SINCE MARIA WAS MURDERED, ARMANDO HAD ANOTHER goal besides finding the bastards who killed the love of his life. Now he was also compelled to help this good-hearted young lady who sat next to him at the small fire. Yes, he would try his best to support her quest for justice, too, if he could ever find a way out of his own hell.

Armando was surprised at her rational way of thinking "You think the judge is connected to the murders, don't you?" She shrugged her shoulders.

Elli ground a fist into her palm. "If you want to help me, we have to first make sure you are off the hook with the law. That's only possible if we find the true killers."

"So, you believe me?" he asked hopefully.

She looked straight into his eyes, and "Yes," was all she said. It was all he needed to hear.

Armando nodded. "Not only is Judge Werdinger the railway owner's brother, but he would become very rich, too, if he owned the properties next to the planned tracks. We had no enemies in town, but he and his brother surely started to behave in nasty ways after I turned down their offers to buy my place couple of times. You know, they put a spoke in the wheel numerous times out at the estancia. I think they let the horses run away to make sure I was gone that fatal day."

"All we have to do is prove they were connected or did the killings themselves, right?"

He laughed but it was a bitter sound. "Easier said than done, lady. But yes, that sums it up pretty much."

"My father taught me that all details matter, so I will ride out to your place and see if I can find any clues that others have overlooked."

Armando seemed impressed with her bravery to even consider entering a house where murders had taken place, but she was right. It would be too risky for him to show up there.

Elli shook her head. "Father always told me to respect the law and the men who represent it. If that judge is really involved in a triple murder case, I will probably end up beating the hell out of him for destroying my childhood beliefs."

The Spaniard stared at her for a moment and then laughed so hard his temples started to hurt. It was his first real laughter since he found his dying wife weeks ago. It felt like a healing medicine warming his heart. He nodded and helped her into the saddle.

She left the rest of her food with him and promised to be back in two days at the latest. He trusted that she would come back alone.

* * *

Elli rode to Armando's ranch. The place was deserted. Thinking about entering a house where three murders had occurred made her nervous.

The home was big and well built, flowers and citrus trees were planted around the perimeter. It would have been a lovely sight if she hadn't known of the cruel deeds that had taken place here. She wrapped Thunder's reins around the hitching pole and slowly climbed onto the porch. Her steps sounded unusually loud in the eerie silence—not even an animal sound. Someone must have removed the livestock.

The interior was dusty and a few chairs were turned over, the signs of the fight that had led to murder weeks ago. Elli walked slowly into the bedroom at the back of the house and prepared herself for the worst. The bed was a mess. How terrible it must have been to find his dying wife lying in her own blood. The gunshot wound must have been huge when judging by the amount of blood on the sheets. The sun filtered through the window, and a glint on the floor just under the bed caught her eye. She bent down, carefully avoiding placing her hands on the linens.

Under the wooden frame she saw a coin on a fragment of gold chain. She retrieved it and turned the coin over in her cold hand. The imprint on the opposite side caused her to cry out in surprise. "That can't be!"

Then the shocked woman quickly placed the coin into her vest pocket where the sheriff's badge retained the warmth of her body.

Elli Townsend walked to the barn, but found no clues there except for the stains of dried blood on the ground and in the hay. But it didn't matter. She had what she needed. Armando Diaz was innocent and Elli knew who the murderer was. She jumped into the saddle and rode straight back to the cave where Armando was hiding.

* * *

Late afternoon the next day after having slept in the cave, Elli rode along the main street right to the sheriff's office. Harris jumped out of his chair as he saw her. "I know where Diaz is hiding!" she started the conversation without even greeting him.

"Oh, that's good news, ma'am. Where is he? I need to send the posse right away to arrest that scalawag."

But Elli shook her head. "I understand the judge is highly interested in capturing the murderer so I suggest I clean up at the hotel, and you tell Mister Werdinger to meet me there in an hour. After all, I want to get the reward since I found the suspect. I could sure use the money."

The sheriff obviously didn't like that.

Elli was quite sure he wanted the reward for himself, but he had to obey the young woman's orders for the moment. He agreed and Elli walked over to the hotel after returning her horse to the Lucky Mule Livery.

She washed herself in the porcelain basin, dressed in a new shirt, and brushed her long hair, trying to look as feminine as possible under the circumstances. She waited for the judge to show up.

Finally, Judge Werdinger knocked at the door of the basic hotel room. Elli opened it and motioned for him to step in. The man had the slanted eyes of a rat, and as a sheriff's daughter, she fought the urge to spit in his face.

"Good evening, Miss Townsend. I'm pleased to finally meet you in person. Sheriff Harris told me you achieved what my posse failed to do—find the murderer of the Diaz family. I must admit you are very much your father's daughter. You definitely got sand, young lady!"

"Thank you, Mister Werdinger. I will provide you the information about where he is hiding, but I want my reward first and a piece of the cake you are expecting soon as well."

He looked puzzled. "What do you mean, ma'am?"

"Well, now that the doors are wide open for you to lay hands on the Diaz property, you will be a very rich man as soon as the railway tracks are finished. That will most likely be in a very short time. Am I right?"

He stared and waited for her to continue her speech. Elli could almost see the wheels turning in his head, as he probably wondered how much she knew about his cutthroat deeds.

"Wasn't that the reason why you killed them, judge?"

"I don't have the slightest idea what you're talking about, young lady."

"Oh, is that so? Well, let me refresh your memory then, Judge Werdinger. It wasn't enough for you to try and steal Armando's land, was it? No, you had to kill his entire family. I would have thought you'd gotten your sheriff or the deputies to do the dirty work for you just like you had them beat Armando up on his way back to California. But no, you even killed his wife by yourself."

* * *

He couldn't believe it. How in the world would she know all this? Never mind, he thought. She would disappear from here and never be seen again; he would take care of this.

"What gives you the idea that I killed the bastard's filly? You have no way to prove this, you silly little Arizonan snot nose."

She stared him straight in the eyes and didn't give an inch. Stretching out her hand, she revealed the cold coin on its chain, and read the inscription in a ringing voice.

"'For my beloved brother, Isaac Werdinger from Jacob Werdinger, the Railway King,'" she intoned.

"You lost it in the very same room where you shot the

poor woman. You are nothing but a corrupt murderer and you deserve to be hanged for it. You'll never abuse the sacred positions of 'judge' or 'the law' ever again. You shall burn in hell, Werdinger, and meet your very own Judge there."

Werdinger turned pale. The coin proved he had been there and most likely shot Armando's wife. He had to get rid of Townsend's daughter right away. She could end his entire career in the blink of an eye and even more, invite him into a necktie party with his own neck in the noose.

"You will not tell this to anybody. Matter of fact, you won't be leaving this room alive. You think you're smart, but you ain't. You called out the wrong person, young missy."

He took a step forward, his hands outstretched as if to strangle her. At that moment the connecting door to the next room flew open and Armando stood in its frame with a shotgun in his hands, his face a mask of pure, raging fury. Werdinger almost lost his balance as he tried to move backwards out the door. His mouth hung open and his eyes were wide in shock at seeing the Spaniard with the gun aiming at his stomach.

Werdinger knew he was a dead man.

The judge called out for the sheriff who was waiting at the entrance area of the hotel. Ruby Hershberger kept Sheriff Harris in check with a double barrel shotgun. She growled at him, "Don't even consider making a move. This time you pulled the wrong bull by its tail, and you and that greedy devil up there are going to face justice, you hear me?"

Harris winced as he stared down the barrel of the loaded gun and the fierce woman holding it. There was no doubt that Ruby would pull the trigger if necessary.

Meanwhile, Armando stood in the door frame, barely able to control his rage. Werdinger stared at him. Elli called out Armando's name, but he didn't hear her.

"You killed my wife!" he screamed at the judge. "I found her in a pool of blood on our bed! I'll make you pay for it!" His finger was on the trigger, and his hand trembled.

Suddenly he felt a soft touch on his arm and looked sideways. Elli stood beside him. "Not here, Armando. He'll hang, we'll see to that. Remember, you have to be free! He *will* face justice, and he will die at the hands of the law."

Armando hesitated, but then lowered the gun and walked over to Werdinger who tried to cower against the wall. Beads of sweat formed on his forehead. Armando pulled his pistol from its holster and in one swift move buffaloed his opponent to the ground.

He called out the name of a rancher friend. "Hank!" It was one of the two gentlemen whose conversation Elli had overheard in Ruby's restaurant the other day. The man had been waiting for Armando's instructions in the adjoining room.

"Let's carry him over to the crowbar hotel before I change my mind and put this scum straight into the bone orchard, Hank." His friend patted him on the shoulder, then bent down and helped him pick up the judge.

CHAPTER SIX

***

THE NEXT DAY ARMANDO AND ELLI ATE LUNCH IN RUBY'S LUCKY POT RESTAU-
rant. The good-looking noble man was very quiet. Elli
patted his hand.

"Your reputation is restored, my dear friend. You can
continue running your ranch and the judge and sheriff will
both face justice. After all, they have admitted to being re-
sponsible for the murders. They even accused each other,"
Elli added shaking her head in dismay.

"It won't bring back my family though," Armando
said. "I spoke to Hank; he'll run the ranch for me for a
little while until I decide what to do with it. I will help
you, like you helped me, to find the rats that killed your
father. After all, without you, I would most likely not be
alive now, Elli."

She waved her hand to shake it off. "Any decent person
would have helped you."

But he disagreed. "No, seriously, Elli. I owe you my life
and will never let you down. We have a mission!"

She searched his gaze, and without a word, they settled
a promise to protect each other.

Elli watched his face closely. He looked tired and pale under his tanned skin. The gash on his temple was healing, but the pain showing in his eyes would take an eternity to fade away, just like hers.

"Well, Mister Diaz, I would say, as soon as we have watched those two jerks dangling from the leafless tree, we have a mission to follow, right?" He smiled back. "Yes, ma'am, we certainly do!"

A few days later both witnessed the hangings of Judge Werdinger and Sheriff Harris. Elli wondered what Armando felt when he saw the two men crying for forgiveness and mercy. She could not believe how shamefully they behaved. "They should at least have the backbone to face the consequences like true men, but I guess they never knew what honor and dignity meant."

Armando Diaz didn't answer. His jawbone was clenched in a tight line. Elli assumed it must be a very emotional moment for him to watch the two murderers of his family face justice and pay for their crimes.

The trapdoor beneath them opened with a loud crash, and both men trembled and jerked on the end of their ropes for a long minutes.

Neither was granted the faster death by breaking their necks, but finally, it was over and their bodies swung back and forth on the two ropes.

Armando closed his eyes for a moment. "Maybe there is justice after all," he whispered. Turning to Elli, he said, "My family members are still gone, Elli, and it still hurts the same."

Turning away, he gave last minute instructions to his friend about how to handle the cattle while he was gone.

***

The next morning Elli saddled Thunder, and Armando walked into the stable to hand her the rifle she had brought along. "You sure you want to do this, Armando?" She still felt insecure about his offer to help her chase her father's murderers.

When he spoke, his voice was grim. "I told you I owe you and will help you. I am a man of honor, Eleonora, have always been. It is the least I can do in return for the way you have saved me. You may not be aware, but before I met you, I hadn't anything to lose. You gave me a part of my life back. Although my Maria and her parents are gone, I still have a future, thanks to you. I just need to learn to live again, without them, but that is something no one can help me with.

"Right now, I can't bring myself to live in the house where they died. Maybe someday."

Elli knew what he meant. Life was never the same after losing a loved one. It would always hurt until one finally closes his or her eyes forever. She prayed that both she and Armando would find peace for their souls ... the peace that was stolen from them as they held their treasured dying family members in their arms.

They were about to mount their horses when they saw Ruby rushing toward them with two cotton sacks thrown over her shoulders. "I reckon you could use some food on the way. You didn't really plan to leave this town without letting me make sure you don't starve on the trail, did you?" They both laughed and thanked her for the offered provisions.

Ruby turned serious. "May God protect you both, and please return soon, you two."

Elli hugged the woman. "Thank you, Ruby, for all you have done. If God grants us success, we shall return soon and healthy."

"It's a dangerous mission you are on, young lady. Make sure it doesn't poison your heart."

"I will try my best, Ruby!"

"There will always be a table waiting for you at my restaurant, Elli. You saved one of my best friends, and I am very grateful for that." Elli blushed and Armando smiled warmly at the elder woman.

They both climbed into their saddles and rode out of town. Some townspeople nodded a respectful greeting.

As they rode toward the Arizona Territory, they spoke about their plan of how they would attempt to find the gang that had ambushed Sheriff Townsend. Unfortunately, Armando had only overheard their first names. He wasn't even certain if they had used their real names when addressing each other. Elli was hoping to hear something in the saloons or brothels around Yuma or other boomtowns such as Tombstone, Goldfield, or Bisbee. They were surely hiding somewhere, but not for long. It would be too tempting to spend their big stack of gold on whiskey and women of easy virtue. Armando was certain that they would show up in one of those boomtowns which were known to be a favorite nest of gamblers, rustlers, and cutthroats.

Elli was relieved to have the good-looking Spaniard for a companion as she knew that those towns were quite dangerous for a pretty young woman travelling alone.

***

The sun stood high; it was past noon and they rode in silence. Elli watched Armando. He seemed lost in his thoughts. Now that his enemies were dead, it left him without a goal, and he felt lonelier and more devastated than ever before. He didn't admit it, but it might have been comforting for him to have Elli at his side. If one person in this entire world understood his pain, it was she. Other women might force a conversation on him, but not her. He watched her, the way she rode, confident and in harmony with the beautiful stallion. It was plain to see how much she loved the magnificent horse. She was indeed special in many ways. But then he lowered his eyes again and concentrated on the trail ahead.

As the sun began to sink, he reined in his horse. "I think we should look for a place to camp. It will be another few days until we are back in Yuma, unless you want to search more toward the south or north of it."

She looked at him, puzzled about his thought. He shrugged his shoulders. "If I were they, I wouldn't linger too long in an area where I shot a lawman and others but would head for an environment where I would find my kind of people and where I could live on the owl hoot trail without bringing attention to myself about the murders."

"You're probably right."

They stopped their tired horses at a small canyon and while she prepared a campfire, Armando tended to his chestnut colored gelding and her stallion.

They enjoyed some of Ruby's meatloaf and the baked biscuits, both hungry and appreciative of the food. Armando got up and searched his saddlebags until he came up with a pot and some coffee and sugar. Elli's eyes grew wide. "Coffee? Really?"

He laughed. "Well, I can't compete with Ruby's cuisine, but at least I can make us some hot, strong coffee." He was glad he had brought it along. It felt good to see her smile. It was rare, but it was a smile that could light up an entire room.

Elli dug deeper into the provisions packed by Ruby.

"I'll be darned!" she exclaimed.

"What is it?"

"Looks like an apple cake!" Now it was Armando's turn to smile. How blessed he was with amazing friends.

They both enjoyed the coffee and cake in silence while the flames crackled and sent sparks against the night sky full of stars.

"I always try to comfort myself by thinking that one of those stars up there is my father, and that he's watching over me" Elli said with a sad smile curling her nicely shaped lips.

"I like that thought" he said. "Maybe I should imagine my beloved Maria and her parents to also be among those twinkling lights up there in heaven."

"By the way, why haven't you married anyone in Yuma yet, Elli? After all, you are a pretty girl." Armando almost bit his tongue for being so blunt.

But she turned and answered him without hesitation. "My Mom and Dad were an amazing couple. They loved and respected each other dearly. I don't want to settle for less just for the sake of getting hitched. Hence, I wait for the right one who earns my trust and conquers my heart the same way my Dad did with Mom."

"Good point there, no need to hurry anyway. After all, you are still young."

She laughed. "We never know how long that might take. Maybe I'll end up being an old maid."

"Ha, I doubt that," he said with a broad smile that changed his handsome masculine features into a boyish face. Finally, they went to sleep next to the campfire. A coyote yipped somewhere close by.

CHAPTER SEVEN

***

AFTER THEIR BREAKFAST OF LEFTOVERS AND COFFEE THEY DECIDED TO START their search in the town of Florence. They knew it would be a three-day ride to get there. Florence was a promising source for information. It was growing quite rapidly—lots of people lived there, and maybe some had seen the scamps.

At first Armando harbored concerns about Elli keeping up with the challenging ride, but, after two days, he had to admit that she was quite a tough cookie. Not once did she complain about the heat or her bones hurting. It was plain to see that his admiration for her spirit grew with each passing hour. Yet Armando tried to redirect some of her energy which was fueled by the most dangerous of all emotions—hatred. He didn't like the idea that the anger and hate she felt for the killers might lead her into danger by taking unnecessary risks.

One evening he told her so. Elli let him she could take care of herself.

When they arrived in Florence they went straight to the rental stables and had their horses fed and watered. They also asked the blacksmith to shoe them freshly if necessary.

Then they walked over to the hotel.

They had agreed to check in as Mr. and Mrs. Gonzalez to make sure they didn't raise any suspicions. Armando could not bring himself to call Elli Mrs. Diaz so soon after his wife's passing and apologized to her about it, but Elli didn't feel offended at all.

After a decent meal and a bath, he walked over to the Tunnel Saloon without Elli. A decent woman would not have walked into such an establishment. Hoping to find out something about the outlaws they were hunting, he ordered a whiskey. It didn't take long before one of the soiled doves tried to charm him into paying for her drink, which he did.

"What brings you into town, handsome?"

He turned toward her, then quickly scanned the men at the poker table. "I'm looking for some friends of mine. Three of them, to be a bit more specific. One has a long scar across his cheek. The other two are brothers with blond curly hair named Pete and Darrell. They told me they would be spending some of the gold they found on some pretty ladies of the night such as you. Seen any of them around Florence lately? Unfortunately, I lost track of them as I got held back in good old California." Armando hoped that his story convinced her.

She looked around the room, then pulled him over to a small table in the corner, taking a bottle of corn liquor and two glasses with her. Armando grew nervous. Did she have some information for him?

"Sit down, stranger, and have another drink with me. Not too many good-looking pals that come into our saloon lately." She poured him a shot, then one for herself and lifted the glass. "To this night which is still young enough to show you paradise, cowboy."

He smiled at her but took only a small sip. She must be

used to drinking a fair amount of the cowboy cocktail as she was about to refill her glass right away.

"They were here," she started without any more sweet-talk. "The man, you are talking about called himself Texas Logan. I remember him well. Had a long scar across his right cheek, just like you said. Must have had a bad argument with the blade of someone's knife some time ago."

"Yep, that is surely him. Were the two brothers with him, Pete and Darrell?"

"You must be talking about the Lenny brothers. As a matter of fact, they were here as well. True, they had some gold to celebrate a few hearty nights. But they left soon after one of the brothers beat up one of my best girls. Poor thing won't be able to work for weeks.

We called the sheriff about it, but show me one law dog that would step up for one of us ladies of the line. No sir, if it had been a townsfolk woman, they would have raised hell, but for us? You know how that story goes."

She let the sentence trail off and he knew she was right. It was one of the sad aspects of life in the red-light district of each boomtown.

"Tell me, you handsome devil, you wouldn't treat a lady like that, would you?"

He shook his head. "Never, but, as a matter of fact, my wife is travelling with me and I'd better get back to where we're staying or she will most likely raise hell tonight. Do you know where those men went after leaving Florence?"

She looked at him, a sad expression on her face. "You know what, stranger, I envy your wife. And no, I don't know where they were heading to, but they spoke about the Northern Territory around Wickenburg a lot. They were making plans to find more gold up there. That's all I know. By the way, you got to pay for the whiskey."

"I will and more than that. Here's some extra pay for the nice conversation. You ought to find yourself a decent husband, ma'am."

She took the money and walked back to the bar. She could not recall the last time a man had addressed her so respectfully by calling her "ma'am."

He somehow seemed to be so different from the cutthroats he was looking for. She started to doubt his story, yet it was none of her business. and with a flattering smile she walked over to her next possible lover for the night. But the smile didn't reach her cold eyes.

* * *

When Armando returned to the hotel, he walked straight to their room. He hung his hat on the hook behind the door and was just about to tell Elli what he had found out, but when he turned, he saw her on the bed. She was sleeping, so he carefully walked over and covered her with the blanket. She mumbled in her sleep and he smiled. She had cleaned herself up as much as possible, and must have brushed her long hair. It covered most of the pillow. For the first time since he had met her in front of her father's office in Yuma, Armando saw her with the eyes of a man and was in awe of her innocent beauty. Then he quickly turned away, took off his boots and jacket, and settled into the rocking chair that stood in the corner of the room.

Next morning, he woke up after having slept only a few hours and stretched his stiff back, wincing at the pain it caused. *Dang, I'm starting to feel my age it seems.*

Elli woke up and immediately blushed. "Oh, my God, did you sleep in that rocking chair all night? You should have woken me and we could have taken shifts for sleeping in the bed."

"Never mind. I just need a strong coffee, bacon and eggs, and I will be a new man," he said and washed his face in the bowl.

As they enjoyed a hearty breakfast together, Armando filled her in with all the details he found out about Texas Logan, as the gang leader was called. "Wickenburg is where we are heading, right?"

Armando shook his head. "Since we are close to Tucson, I would like to visit a friend of mine there. He's a retired marshal and still hears a lot through the grapevine. I want to make sure that word gets to us in case the gang decides to move south again. Most of them steal or sell cattle across the border. That alright with you?"

She agreed immediately. "Whatever helps us capture them, you can count me in."

* * *

An hour later they were on the trail to Tucson. By early evening they arrived. Armando's friend, a former marshal of Swedish heritage, greeted them happily.

"Larson, so good to see you, pal."

"Armando, what brings you out here to the dry desert away from your lush paradise?"

He glanced curiously at Elli. "Where is Maria?"

Armando sat and quickly told his friend the story about what had happened back in Orange Grove.

Larson's face was full of sympathy. "I'm so sorry, my dear friend. What a cruel path your life has taken. But since the judge and that crooked sheriff were executed, what brings you here?"

Armando looked at Elli. He explained to Larson that Elli faced a similar destiny and that they were on the hunt for the murderers of her late father.

"Oh, you're talking about Sheriff Oscar Townsend? He was your father? God bless his soul. Fine lawman, he was. We once rode together. I'm honored to meet his daughter."

Elli Townsend smiled at the man with tears pooling in her eyes. "Have you seen the outlaws by any chance?" she asked hopefully.

"Hell, I think one-third of Arizona is either involved in robberies or cattle rustling. Most of them along the frontier are following the owl hoot trail one way or the other, up to no-good." But then Larson scratched his chin.

"Well, two weeks ago a prospector named Ronan Mc-Dowry came into town for some goods and told me a story that he ran into three dangerous looking guys. They more or less forced him to share his campfire and all his food provisions with them. Most likely, the fact that he even shared his precious Irish whiskey probably saved his life. However, one of the guys bragged that he wasn't even scared of the devil himself. He spilled the beans that he had shot a sheriff not too long ago. The prospector said the leader had a long scar running across his right cheek. Might be the guy you're looking for, young lady. The miner said that the other two mentioned they were brothers. Sounds like the fellows you're after."

"Texas Logan," Elli whispered. He was the man she hated with all her heart. The cold-blooded murderer who had taken away the most important human being in Elli's life.

Armando gently touched her shoulder. "We will get him and the others, too. We will make them pay. I promise!" She swallowed away her tears.

CHAPTER EIGHT

***

THE GHOSTS SHE HAD STARTED TO HUNT WEEKS AGO NOW HAD NAMES AND more than one witness who could identify them had been found. Even more so, they might be able to trace where they rode when they left Florence. Yes, they were on their tail.

Armando watched her closely, so did former Marshal Larson. Both men understood her expression which bore pure hunger for revenge. It was the look of a killer.

"Where do we find that prospector?" she asked Larson.

"He left town, but as far as I understood, his claim is not too far from here toward the Mule Mountains. I can write down directions for you. I think he ordered some goods from the local mercantile, and I'm certain the owner there has the exact location as he delivers to the miners. Earns him quite a bit of extra hard money to provide that service with his wagon."

The next day Armando and Elli convinced the owner of the local mercantile to let them deliver the goods to the miner's claim. They just needed information as to where the man could be found. Elli told a tale about being the prospector's younger sister and was even willing to pay the delivery fee. The mercantile owner didn't mind at all that he wouldn't need to travel out there through the rugged country and happily agreed.

He gave them the sack of coffee, bags of sugar and flour, as well as the black powder and jerky the man had ordered. They were able to pack a few cans of beans, canned peaches, and a slab of bacon.

Elli and Armando rode out of town following the directions to the Irishman's claim right in the middle of the Mule Mountains. They rode along a stream that led to his camp.

Once again Elli was so grateful for having Armando by her side. Slowly but surely, she realized that she would have never gotten this far hunting for the Logan gang all by herself.

After another half hour's ride along the shallow creek they found a crude cabin which was most likely McDowry's. They called out his name. He was behind the cabin washing his long johns in the cold gurgling water of the creek. He was astonished to see the two visitors approaching on their horses.

"Howdy folks, what brings you out here"? As he asked the question, he glanced at the rifle leaning against the frame of his simple cabin.

Armando followed his glance. "You don't need to worry, sir. We only came here to ask you about some people you may know, and we brought your goods from the mercantile in Tucson."

The confusion on McDowry's face was clearly visible. "I'm sorry, I didn't expect guests, but I might be able to offer some coffee to you fellows, I mean, sorry, ma'am."

Elli smiled and handed him the bag of coffee and sugar while Armando emptied the other saddlebags. "I'm sure glad to see those goods. I was running out of most, but to run out of coffee is the worst, I tell you! So, what is it you need to know from me?"

"Mister McDowry," Elli started but he interrupted her. "Call me Ronan, please. I don't believe much in formalities."

"Alright, Ronan then. I am Elli Townsend and this is Armando Phillipe Diaz. Had any luck finding gold so far? Your cabin looks like you're prepared to stay for quite a while on this claim."

The Irishman shrugged his shoulders. "Only God knows where He will lead me next."

Armando raised an eyebrow. He pointed over to the Bible on the table. "I see that you are a man with respect for the Good Book, Ronan."

The man busily prepared the coffee and nodded eagerly. "Actually, I am a priest." Elli and Armando exchanged looks of surprise. "I know it sounds kind of out of place, a gold-digging priest."

McDowry set down some old tin cups and poured them all fresh, steaming coffee. With a small boy's broad smile, he put an extra spoon of sugar into his and handed around the sugar bag.

"Ronan, a friend of Armando told us you met some rowdy folks before you went to Tucson for your provisions. I need to find those men."

Armando followed the conversation silently, stirring his coffee.

"Well, lady, I don't think a pretty young thing like you should ever have anything to do with them. They seemed dangerous and they didn't even try to hide that they're outlaws. If you ask me, I was lucky to have survived that night."

Elli nodded. "I want to be straight forward. I have reason to believe that these men killed my father."

The priest scratched his chin for a moment. "I see, I get your point and, although we just met, it seems you are not the kind of woman to be stopped very easily."

Armando smiled at that statement as though he whole-heartedly agreed.

Ronan went on. "One of the men was called Texas Logan. He has dark, shoulder length hair and a mustache. Average height and pretty slim, I would say. His eyes are piercing, dark like my coffee, almost black, and when he looks at you with those eyes, it gives you the chills, I swear. Oh, and he has a long fire-red scar running across his right cheek. Must have had a run-in with an enemy's knife. His two compadres seemed to be brothers. I think their names were Pete and Darrell Lenny, at least those were the names they used.

"Both have curly blond hair. It was getting dark the time they came to my camp, but they both have blue eyes, if I'm not mistaken. Same size and figure as myself, I would say. It was easy to see that Texas Logan is the boss of the gang. If you ask me, he's a cold-blooded killer."

***

Armando looked worried. *This crazy woman really wants to follow three dangerous renegades. Dang, she might not know what she's getting herself into,* he mused while staring into his tin cup.

Elli pressed their host. "Do you know where they went?"

"They spoke about heading north to the Wickenburg territory, something about they had some business to do in Jerome as well. They were kind of cautious about spilling too much about their whereabouts, it seemed."

Elli looked into Armando's worried face. "Wickenburg is reconfirmed, I would say." Her companion didn't argue against it.

McDowry motioned for them to wait. "Actually, since you have been honest with me, I want to tell you the truth about myself, folks. I'm not really digging for gold. Well, I am but not in the way you would think. As I told you, I am a priest. I followed a family member's letter all the way from Ireland to the Wild West here. My late great-grand uncle, whose name was Buen Tio Don as the Spanish nicknamed him for "Good Uncle Don," started a beautiful hacienda in this territory. I intend to find it and rebuild it to its former glory. That's why I was hoping to find some gold here as I could use the money to do so."

"I assume you know where your family member's estate could be found since you have a letter describing it," Armando said.

"Well, Armando, the letter got lost, you see. We finally found it years later in the belongings of my late father. It was over twenty years ago that the 'Garden of Solitude,' as the hacienda had been named, was in its splendor. The exact location is not known to anybody anymore."

"Why this specific ranch? There are plenty for sale out here and if you get lucky finding some gold you can buy whatever ranch you want," Armando suggested.

"See, the point is my relative must have been very friendly with local Indians and they traded with him in turquoise, silver, and even gold. That is all described in the letter. The wealth of the hacienda must have been enormous. He even built a small mission and chapel on his land.

"My relative wrote about that mission chapel. He mentioned that the altar was decorated with figures of the four evangelists made out of solid gold. I've traveled through Arizona for over a year now, trying to find out more, but nobody seems to know about the place. All I know is that it was in Arizona territory in a certain area. Do not misunderstand my intentions. I want to bring the mission back to life, or at least the gold figures back to their homeland church, and continue the missionary work that he started during the heydays of the estancia."

Elli looked skeptical; the story sounded too fantastic. Gold and lost treasure were fairytales which you could hear at the campfires throughout the Wild West.

It was easier to convince Armando. Being of old Spanish blood, he knew very well how much gold and treasures the Spanish had collected, and obviously the Irish ancestor of McDowry must have had some connection to leading Spaniards in the area or he would not have carried the Spanish nickname.

"Are you sure you're not just on the hunt for the treasure for your own purposes?" Elli called him straight out.

Again, Armando face showed astonishment about her backbone, but he wondered about the true motives of the priest as well. McDowry got up and took the Bible off the table. He didn't seem to be offended.

"I understand your doubts. Our entire village would have starved to death if my ancestor hadn't sent a ship full of goods, he was able to buy with the help of the Indian gold. I would never betray his trust. I want to continue what he started for the sake of honoring him and continuing the good deeds he did in my home country. After all, things are tough again in old Ireland. I hear of the starving children there and it is heart breaking. I believe that faith has brought that letter to me."

Armando looked at him. "Even if you find that place and, what is even more questionable, if the gold is still there, do you really believe you can easily walk through the frontier with a fortune in your saddlebags? You would not survive a single week. This territory is packed with murderers, cutthroats, cattle rustlers, even corrupted lawmen, to name but a few."

"If I'm in such danger, why don't we ride together? The place is said to be northwest from here. The hunt for those men leads you in the direction of north anyway. That way we could have each other's back. And who knows, you may hear more about the Logan gang on the trail."

Armando thought about it. He didn't like it, but it wasn't a bad idea to have another man by his side to protect Elli.

Elli looked thoughtful. "If anything about a hidden treasure leaks, we would encounter outlaws pretty quick. But then it might even shake up the Logan gang and play them right into our hands. What do you think, Armando?"

"It is a risky game, Elli. The Logan gang is dangerous, but, by God, they are not the only ones in this area. It's your mission to find your father's murderers so I leave the decision up to you. Whatever you decide, I'm in. I always stand by my word, Elli."

"Let's ride together then. We'll start at daylight."

With that said, they helped McDowry pack some provisions, gathered his horse and mule, and prepared to ride out of at sunrise.

***

Their way led them right back to Armando's friend Larson in Tucson. Before they left Tucson to ride north toward Wickenburg, Larson had promised to keep them informed via telegraph if any of the gang members showed up there. He pulled Elli aside while Armando and McDowry spoke about the next day's route.

"I understand that you have to do what you got to do, but make sure I see your beautiful face again one day. Hatred and revenge are not the best guides for a hand that needs good aim. When the day comes that your gun shall fulfill your revenge, then make sure you let your brains lead your action, and not your heart full of pain and fury. If you don't control your emotions, never mind how painful they may be, you will die. Do you understand what I'm saying?"

"Yes, sir, I do, and I'm grateful for your advice." Elli hugged the man.

Armando watched them from the other side of the room.

"We shall see each other again one day, Mister Larson. I always make it a point to keep my promises." She patted him on the shoulder and thanked him again.

CHAPTER NINE

* * *

AS THE THREE RODE OUT OF THE TOWN, MCDOWRY ADMITTED THAT HE INDEED had an old map of the area where his relative's estancia was supposed to be located.

"Where in the world did you find this map and why haven't you found the place by yourself?"

Armando's question sounded suspicious, but he didn't bother to apologize. He and Elli both had doubts about the story of the lost treasure.

"Well, I am sorry, Armando, but you must understand that I had to make sure that you really believe me at all. I have to be careful to whom I tell that story and giving too much information to the wrong folks would most likely get me straight to the nearest undertaker. Besides, I don't know how accurate the map is."

Elli and Armando studied the faded piece of paper. According to the map the hacienda was positioned north of Tucson. "That looks like right in the middle of nowhere. Why would anybody build a ranch up there?"

"My great-grand uncle worked for the Spanish in Mexico for quite a while; that's how he got the nickname

Buen Tio Don. They gave him that piece of land after his service was no longer needed. Maybe they wanted to make sure he was as far away as possible from their unmarried daughters." McDowry chuckled. "However, he describes the place as the 'Garden of Solitude.' "

Way past noon the three rested for a meal next to a rock formation. It provided some shade welcomed by the horses and their sweaty riders. Again, they studied the map. "That ridge on the left of the hacienda called Picacho Rock is shaped kind of unusually," remarked Elli.

After they finished a meal of dry bread and beef jerky, Armando watered the horses from his extra flask before getting back into their saddles. They could reach the Picacho Rock and camp there for the night if they hurried.

When the group got closer to the area, they were impressed by the shape of the rock formation. It resembled a pyramid or a broken-off tooth of some ancient giant. But there was no sign at all that there had been a hacienda or a chapel. No building was visible in the area east of the formation. They realized that this side of the geological sight was rather sandy at the foot of it, and they were cautious to make sure they would not get caught in quicksand.

Fortunately, there was some tumbleweed and dry wood close by for a campfire, and the rock gave them shelter against a chilly wind that had blown in from west. The Picacho's nearly vertical wall reflected the day's heat, and a little campfire kept them warm.

"The soil isn't as hard baked here like in the rest of the territory, is it?" said Armando while he poked his knife into the loose sand.

"There seems to be a thick layer of sand." McDowry looked at him thoughtfully.

"I assume it gets blown into this corner when it's windy.

After all, they have real dust storms here."

Armando nodded. "You're probably right! I guess that big rock blocks the dust and sand, and it trickles down to the ground here at this cliff, building a thick sandy cushion. It'll make the ground softer to sleep on. Just be sure you check your boots in the morning. For me this looks like scorpion country, and I don't want to be stung on my foot."

Ronan grew pale. He wasn't yet used to the adventure and dangers of the Wild West.

Elli laughed at his expression. Then she lay down, head on her saddle.

It was long after midnight, and the stars were shining their eternal light down onto the quiet desert country. A lonely coyote howled at the moon, barely visible behind the clouds that had moved in with the wind.

The air was chilly and the fire had burned down. Elli opened her eyes but couldn't say what woke her. It was a sound that didn't fit in this area. She couldn't name it, but it reminded her of childhood days. She listened carefully. The two men seemed to be deeply asleep. There it was again, a soft chime, but Elli couldn't place it at all. As fast as it came, it disappeared again. *Must have been the wind,* she thought.

Elli had trouble going back to sleep. Finally, she fell into a shallow slumber.

When she woke Armando was already poking the fire back to life, and Ronan was praying in silence a few feet away.

"Good Morning Elli, sleep well?" Armando looked at her, waiting for an answer.

Elli rubbed the sleep from her eyes. "No, not at all, I woke up in the middle of the night, heard a weird sound and couldn't go back to sleep after that. It bothers me that

I can't place it."

"What did it sound like?" McDowry had walked back to them and prepared strong cowboy coffee over the fire.

"I can't name it; somehow it sounded muffled but reminded me of something I had heard as a child when father once took me to a bigger town. Something like a very high tone that vibrated but was soft."

She tossed her tangled dark hair back over her shoulder. The two men pondered this information, but Armando shrugged his shoulders. He didn't know what to make of it.

"Wait a minute!" The priest stared at her, then gestured around. "Was it like a chiming sound?"

She nodded. "Somehow, I'm not sure. I was half asleep when I heard it, and it wasn't very clear or loud."

"A bell, could it have been a bell?"

Elli stared at McDowry. "I'll be darned, if that's not possible. Now I remember what it reminded me of. My father took me to a town back in Texas when I was a child, and there was a church with a small bell. The faint sound of that bell followed us out of town."

"Yes, it is possibly a bell, but where in the world would that sound come from? After all, we are in the middle of nowhere." Armando picked up a fistful of sand and let it run through his fingers.

McDowry shrugged his shoulders. "All I know is that my great-grand uncle built a mission chapel around here. Most likely it had a bell to call the people at the mission together for prayers."

Armando followed their conversation, wordlessly playing with the loose sand, when it suddenly struck him.

"Hey, wait a minute, you two! Ronan, you said your great-grand uncle had a thriving hacienda with trees and gardens and the whole works. He was running it like a farm or ranch so it had to be a place that had ground water and shelter to make sure it wasn't exposed to the sun year-round."

"I would think so," agreed the priest, not knowing what Armando was getting at.

Elli looked at her Spanish friend. "I don't get it, why is that important?"

"Well, what if the hacienda was right here?"

Elli laughed. "I don't see any walls, do you?"

"As a rancher, I would have selected this place. The rock cliff gives shelter and the hot afternoon sun is on the other side of the ridge; rain clouds might get caught on this cliff, which means better chances for rain, necessary in this dry land."

"But there is nothing here. We should at least see some adobe walls, shouldn't we?" The priest shook his head, doubting Armando's idea.

"The sand here was blown in by many dust storms; it is loose. See, you can easily lift it up, so that means it's not hard baked desert ground.

What if, layer by layer, inch by inch, it had been blown in here right on top of that hacienda and has slowly but surely buried it under the desert's sand? You said the place was built decades ago."

McDowry and Elli both pondered that thought. "Are you trying to tell us I could have heard that bell chime because the chapel might still be intact and hidden right under our camp? That is absolutely ridiculous, Armando!"

"Maybe so, but it would explain why nobody has found the place and its gold yet, wouldn't it?"

McDowry slowly nodded. "It would explain a hell of a lot if you ask me. Oh, excuse me. I should watch my language." He got up and walked over to his horse, removing the shovel from behind his saddle.

"You felt it like a vibrating sound, Elli, right?"

"Yes, very weak, but I felt the vibration."

"So why don't we give it a try around where you slept?" He started to dig right next to Elli's blanket. The sand was loose and it didn't take much effort. The other two got up and joined him.

After about an hour they were not only dusty and coughing but had also struck a piece of solid rock. It was flat and clearly had been hand chiseled.

"This is absolutely crazy," Elli mumbled.

CHAPTER TEN

***

THEY FOLLOWED THE OUTLINE OF THE CHISELED STONE AND FREED A FLAT ROCK foundation the size of a small house. McDowry shouted, "My God, it might not be a foundation but a roof of solid rocky material. Listen to this!" He hit the handle of his shovel on the exposed area and a hollow echo came back.

"Jesus, there must be a room underneath," Armando exclaimed.

"Yes," the priest said with a smile. "Perhaps we should call upon His help."

The two men tried to lift part of the material and, by using the shovel and a dead branch, a piece of the rock came loose and they were able to lift it up. A big dark hole stared back at them and a breeze of stale, dusty air escaped the darkness underneath with a hiss.

Armando stared at Elli, who was speechless. Was it really possible? Had they found the hidden chapel or the hacienda itself?

McDowry was exuberant, rocking on his heels, whooping, and waving his hat. He lit a branch and waved it through the opening to shine more light into the dark room underneath.

"It really looks like a chapel!" he exclaimed.

"I guess, since I'm the slimmest, I'll have to climb down," Elli suggested. " I'll tie a rope around my waist. Armando, can you hold on to it and make sure I don't fall?"

"Of course."

He knew she could never be convinced not to climb down, so he didn't even try to stop her. The Spaniard got his rope off his saddle, and Elli wrapped it around her small waist, securing it with a tight knot. From a kneeling position, she cautiously lowered herself over the edge of the opening. Armando held tight to the rope while the pretty woman followed the single light beam shining through the hole from the bright daylight above. When Elli touched the ground, she saw that the building was only about double her height. McDowry quickly prepared a torch with a piece of dry saguaro wood and threw it down to her. Elli spun around with the new source of light in her shaking hand. She jumped when she encountered a nest of scorpions.

Fortunately, she had worn her boots. She moved carefully and assumed that snakes could be down there as well.

"What do you see, Elli"? She heard the priest's impatient voice from above.

"Are you okay, Elli?" She smiled at the concern in Armando's voice. "Want scorpions for breakfast?" she hollered back, the echo of her voice booming off the surrounding walls and sending down trickles of sand from the opening through which she had entered.

She walked slowly forward, scaring away spiders and scorpions. There was a slight shimmer across the space. The place was indeed a chapel, about twenty feet long. She had come down from the roof near the rear wall. At the other end She could see an altar. It was a big rock chiseled into a crude cube. Candle holders lay on the floor, and some of the paintings on the walls had been scorched. Black spots marked the walls where the fire had smoldered, but the building appeared intact. No wonder, as it had been built out of solid rock. The air smelled stale.

Slowly her steps took her to the altar. Two skeletons loomed out of the darkness in her torch light. She recoiled and shrieked, startled by the sight. Elli cursed under her breath and tried to calm her racing heartbeat.

"What have you found?" McDowry yelled down into the opening.

"Quit yelling. I don't want this ceiling to collapse on me, you fool! Treasure hunters are down here!" she murmured, then took a closer look at the skeletons. One still wore his clothes, although the boots and hat were gone. The bones had belonged to a tall man.

The other person was covered in what appeared to have been a native female's dress. The position of the bones suggested that the man had tried to protect the woman with his body.

An arrow was lodged in his ribcage. "You got killed by one Indian while you tried to protect another, didn't you?"

Elli shook her head at the sight of this irony. Then a soft glow caught her eye as she moved the torch. The feeling as if someone was watching her gave her the chills. When Sheriff Townsend's daughter turned back toward the rock in the center of the chapel, she saw them. There were four pairs of eyes staring back at her, almost accusingly.

She walked closer to the edge of the altar which wasn't anything more than a squared-off boulder. An iron cross lay in the middle of the stone and to either side of it stood two evangelists, beautifully crafted sculptures so delicately shaped, they almost looked real.

All four figures were less than a foot tall, and when she moved the flame closer, she saw the warm yellow shimmer under a coat of dust. She carefully touched one and wiped away some of the dust with her hand. The warm shine of pure gold made her catch her breath. "Sweet Jesus, I don't believe it. The greenhorn has told us the truth."

"Armando!" she called back. Immediately she could see his head appear in the opening.

"What's wrong, did you find something?"

"Yes, two dead people and some statues. Drop me one of the blankets, and I'll wrap them so you can pull them up with the rope."

A minute later he lowered the bundle. The figures were surprisingly heavy. She treated them with care, placing them in the middle of the blanket and attaching the four corners with a tight knot to the rope. After the precious load had been pulled up by the men, it was her turn.

Armando and McDowry pulled her back into the glaring daylight which blinded her for the first few moments. She drew in some deep breaths of fresh air.

McDowry stared at her, not even daring to touch the blanket. "Well, Ronan, looks like we found your ancestor's place."

She watched him pointing his fingers toward his chest, moving them slowly as he crossed himself.

"You know, I think the hacienda got burned down; the only reason why the chapel still stands is because they built it out of solid rock. God only knows how they achieved that out here."

She pointed to the blanket. "There is the proof that the chapel really existed."

The priest knelt down and with shaky fingers slowly unknotted the bundle. "Holy Trinity!" he exclaimed as he looked at the shining figures.

Even Armando was speechless.

"Buen Tio Don's treasure," McDowry whispered. Elli watched him closely. She had often seen how the common greed for gold changed the facial expressions of men, but this man kneeling on the ground looked at the figures with reverence, and tears filled his eyes.

Armando didn't fall for the spell of the gold either. He was rich himself and yet had lost the greatest treasure in his life. Nothing could touch the man's desire anymore, it seemed. "Ronan, there is something else down there," Elli gently touched the priest's shoulder.

"There are two bodies, one of a tall man and the other, an Indian woman. Indians killed them, it seems, and it looks like he tried to protect her when they died. He was shot by an arrow."

"Armando, could you please keep an eye on the evangelists while I go with Elli? I want to see if I can identify the skeletons."

Armando motioned him to go down into the chapel.

He understood all too well that to let go of heartache, one must face the reality. He securely lowered one after the other down into the long-forgotten chapel, but sweated more when the heavy-set priest hung from the rope.

McDowry trusted the quiet Spanish fellow not to run away with the treasure. He knew Diaz would never leave Elli Townsend.

She walked ahead, slowly leading him to the two victims in front of the altar. He kneeled down while she held the torch to provide some light.

The priest said a prayer. He slowly touched the bones and pulled the arrow out of the rib cage, tossed it away. Then he hesitated. Elli noticed a glint from the dead man's collar. McDowry carefully touched the bones and raised a necklace in his shaking fingers. He twisted it around the bony neck and opened the clasp.

The Irish priest pulled tenderly not wanting to disturb the fragile bones. At the end of the necklace a small silver cross appeared in the dim light of the torch. He turned it around. On the backside, the initials P. McD. were engraved.

"Patrick McDowry, his original name," whispered Ronan. He held the necklace with the tiny cross in his fist while the tears freely rolled down his cheeks. The priest turned away embarrassed, but Elli touched his arm and walked away as far as the dark room allowed. She judged he needed space to mourn his great-grand uncle and the Indian woman who apparently must have been very close to him.

Ronan McDowry looked at the two skeletons. He blessed them and spoke a funeral prayer. Then he put the cross around his own neck and slowly turned toward the rope. A moment later they were pulled up back to the surface of the Arizona desert. There was a moment of silence as they all sat around the campfire, brewing a pot of coffee. The bundle with the gold figures lay next to the silent servant of the church.

"What will you do now?" Elli asked carefully.

"It doesn't make sense to build up the hacienda again. This place is the place of sadness and murder, and I want to close the opening and shovel back the sand. May the two rest in peace down there forever. It's at least a decent burial site, and most likely, they won't be disturbed again. I'll take the figures to his home village, and we'll build a new church in his name, with the help of God. That way the people can always remember him. His legacy of a peaceful mission will continue to live in his original home country."

It was easy to see that Armando's respect for this man grew with each passing hour. He didn't show any sign of wanting to keep the wealth they had just found for himself.

"How in the world do you plan to make it back safely all the way to the East Coast and then catch a ship to Ireland? You are a greenhorn. They will kill you right away if you try it alone!"

McDowry wrinkled his forehead. "You're right, Spaniard. I hardly have a chance to make it. But I don't know anybody in this country so I have to give it a try alone."

Elli thought about it. "We can accompany you to a big fort in the territory, and maybe you can find someone to hire from there."

After pondering that thought for a few minutes they finally agreed and decided to ride toward the closest army post they could find. They also hoped to hear more about the renegades they sought.

They sealed the secret chapel, and McDowry said one last prayer, leaving the two people buried in each other's arms for eternity. Then the travel companions packed the golden figures carefully, dividing them among their saddlebags, and rode off with one last glance in the direction of the majestic Picacho Mountain.

Toward the early evening they arrived in a small town named Swilling's Mill, north of Tucson and stayed in a boarding house. "Let's share a room, Ronan" Armando suggested. "We have to take shifts guarding the gold and Elli needs to get some decent sleep anyway."

So far, the three appeared like normal travelers, but when they got closer to folks, people wondered about them—a handsome foreigner, a man of the Bible, and a beautiful female traveling together were enough reason to cause them to whisper.

The three companions preferred not to stay any longer than necessary to avoid people getting too curious.

CHAPTER ELEVEN

***

THEIR NEXT DESTINATION WAS FORT WHIPPLE, NORTHEAST OF THE ARIZONA.
This was the largest fort in the area and functioned as a kind of capitol for the whole territory. They covered the distance to the fort without interference, but all three were growing nervous, knowing they carried a fortune in gold. People were killed for much less than that. They hadn't heard anything about Texas Logan and his men, but they also didn't want to attract attention to themselves by asking too many questions about that gang. Armando was quite sure these outlaws were known in the area.

At the end of the third day since leaving the hidden chapel, they finally arrived at Fort Whipple. It was a big outpost with buildings constructed from Ponderosa pine and dangerous-looking cannons pointing toward every possible direction where an attack by Indians might originate.

There were military quarters, and some women lived in the fort, mainly the wives of the higher ranking officers. Outside the fort were many tents and brush shelters built from branches and inhabited by natives who had surrendered to the Army.

One of the sergeants welcomed them and showed them where they could find a bed for the night. Armando couldn't help but recognize the lecherous looks of a few of the soldiers on guard when Elli rode by. White women, after all, were rare out here. He didn't like the situation at all and had to keep an eye on her as well as on the priest with his gold statues. *Oh Lord, I feel like I'm watching over a bunch of toddlers.*

After they had eaten a meal of beans and salty bacon, they were shown to an empty bunkhouse with three beds covered with faded wool blankets. Some women invited Elli to sleep in their quarters. But she decided to remain with the two men, which caused some gossip. After the meal Elli took a walk around the fort. When she returned, she carried a tin and two brushes hidden in a shawl.

"What in the world is that for?" asked Armando.

"Ronan, this is some barn color I got from the local trader. You might as well paint those statues with it so nobody sees they are made of gold."

McDowry clapped his hands at the idea. "You are one smart sheriff's daughter. I have to grant you that."

"While you do your work here, I'll walk around and talk to some folks. Maybe I'll run into some information about that Texas Logan scum." Armando grabbed his hat and stepped into the bright sun light.

The good-looking Spaniard stopped at the blacksmith's workshop. "Howdy partner, lots of work?"

"Always. Either I have to shoe horses or they want some iron chain to shackle renegade Indians or bars for the prison carriage."

The smithy was a rough-looking guy with huge arms. Armando watched him hammering a piece of metal that shone with the red color of embers. Sparks flew around the hot material.

"Must be pretty safe to live in a fort," he mused aloud.

"It is but sometimes you can also run into the wrong people here."

The smithy tossed the bent metal into a bucket of dirty water where it cooled down in a hissing cloud of steam.

"Do you encounter outlaws out here? I mean, I am kind of worried about the lady that travels along with us." Armando quickly explained his question.

"Not here lately, but a pack of three robbed a bank close by west of here in the Jerome area a few days ago."

"A gang of three?"

"Yeah, two brothers and their boss man, as they said. Shot the bank employee in cold blood and rode off. They're said to be bunked in this northern area, but the Army and the sheriff of Jerome haven't found them yet. They seem to be smarter than other outlaws."

"Well, I will bring my horse by tomorrow. I'd might like you to check his hooves, sir," said Armando and tipped his hat, then returned to the cabin to report what he had learned.

They seemed to be on the right track toward Texas Logan, but somehow that scamp was always a step ahead. That left Armando even more concerned about how the Irish could bring his evangelists safely on board a sailing ship and back to Ireland.

It almost appeared as if Armando's life had developed an enormous number of unfulfillable tasks lately. While walking back to his travel companions, he muttered to himself, "Why in God's name has my life taken this dramatic turn?" But Armando was a man who stood by his word, and he intended to keep his promise to Elli.

When he entered the bunkhouse, the statues stood on the table with a layer of drying paint on them; they almost looked like regular clay figures.

Armando filled in his friends on what he had discovered regarding Texas Logan and his men. Elli rushed to the door.

"I have to follow them; they might escape again if I don't!" But Armando held her back, trying to calm her down and pointed out the danger of running into the mob unprepared.

***

The priest remained silent. He knew he should help this lady with her hunt for those killers, but he simply couldn't. The chances that he could participate in the chase without drawing attention to the statues were almost zero.

No, it was too risky. He owed his ancestor who had saved the entire village from starving. He needed to bring the statues back and build a future mission in his name. So far, he didn't even know how to get to the East Coast and onto a sailing ship alive.

***

Armando pondered the situation of both of his companions.

He knew nobody could stop Elli Townsend on her path of revenge and understood that well.

The Spanish noble man would have done the same if he were in her shoes. He had actually been in her shoes and knew her feelings of violation well.

Despite the fact that she was a woman, Armando judged her chances of not getting killed by outlaws as better than those of the priest. She was intelligent enough to handle them carefully, and he knew that being a sheriff's daughter, she would most likely never underestimate an outlaw's killer instinct. However, Armando wasn't too sure about the Irish greenhorn, and how long that one would survive out here in the territory. Being an honest man, Armando mentioned those thoughts to the other two in the cabin.

Elli looked at both men. "We should split up," she said calmly.

McDowry's head jerked around. Her friend's face bore an expression of disbelief.

"Armando, I think you should accompany Ronan for a while, at least until he reaches the Texas area and a safe train to New York where he can take a ship back to Ireland."

The handsome Spaniard jumped from his chair. "You can't be serious. I promised to help you find the murderers. And you know it would be your death to encounter the three cutthroats alone." Armando was upset with her and raised his hands as if to shake some sense into her. The preacher ran his fingers through his hair; he hated to be the reason for this argument. The two had been nice to him.

Elli tried to remain calm. "Listen, I will only follow their trail, and you can bring Ronan at least over the Texas border. Once that's done, we'll meet up again, and you can help me catch Logan and the Lenny brothers so we can see them hang."

Armando shook his head. "How in the world do you think I could find you again if we separated now?"

"Telegraph, it's the easiest way. I will return to this very fort and check for a message from you, let's say, three weeks from tomorrow. That way I can wire back to you and let you know where we should meet. I am a sheriff's daughter, and my father knew lawmen in this part of the territory. I can always ask for their help."

Armando shook his head. He didn't like this, no, he didn't like it the least bit, but he knew she was right. Elli Townsend had a better chance of making it on her own than this inexperienced greenhorn next to him with all those gold statues in his saddlebags.

***

McDowry was torn between emotions. On one hand, he was relieved not to have to ride through this harsh territory without any protection, but on the other hand he disliked being the cause of the argument between Elli and Armando. He liked both, and his feeling of guilt and uselessness tore him up. His shoulders slumped and he wrung his hands.

***

The following morning Armando was upset and quiet. He and Elli went over to the cook shack and ate their breakfast in silence. He couldn't tell her what she should do. She was on a mission, and he understood her feelings. Armando already told her that he was truly afraid she would get herself killed. And it bothered him even more that he cared so much for her safety. He looked down at the ground, embarrassed.

He spoke at last. "It feels like a betrayal of my late wife Maria, but I can't help being scared something might happen to you, Elli."

***

Elli was buried in deep thought and knew it looked like she wanted to get rid of Armando, but that wasn't the case. She enjoyed his company more than she would ever admit, even to herself.

But Elli was also an experienced woman of the law and she knew that Ronan would never reach the East Coast alive on his own. Once again, the pretty yet stubborn woman tried to reason with Armando to convince him to accept her plan.

"Well, it is your decision, Elli. I will not argue against it. We will separate then." His manner was cool now and she regretted that the talk went in this direction.

"I'll wait, I promise, I really need your help to capture

that pack of scum. I won't take away your chance to keep your promise to me."

The Spaniard finished his breakfast and got up. "The earlier I hit the trail, the faster that greenhorn sin buster and his gold figures are safe. Excuse me, I should make sure he prepares for the ride and get my horse's shoes checked over at the smithy."

He walked away without looking at her. Obviously, his emotions were in a turmoil. He opened the door to the bunkhouse and informed McDowry that they would ride in an hour. When Elli returned to their accommodation the two men had packed up their few belongings and were ready to leave.

Sheriff Townsend's daughter didn't speak with Armando, but she accompanied them to the stable where they got the horses' hooves checked by the blacksmith. Finally, with a slight delay, they were ready to hit the trail.

"I will ride toward the town of Wickenburg or Prescott and see if I can find where those road agents are hiding," Elli told Armando.

He didn't answer, simply nodded, and checked his cinch, then walked his horse out of the stable. For some reason Elli felt the urge to hold him back. Their Irish companion sensed her discomfort and walked his horse away from the stable, leaving them alone for a moment.

Armando stood there, looking at her. For the first time since meeting her in Yuma he didn't know what to say. *Lord, does she have to look so pretty?* He swallowed and waited, staring at the ground.

"Listen, I will not take any action before you return to help me. When you are ready to come back, let me know." Somehow the words sounded like she meant it in more than one way about waiting for him. He tried to read her expression but didn't dare to ask about it.

When she turned away, he called after her.

"Elli, I can't stop you, but I want you to know that I do not want to find you dying like I found my late wife. You know I care for you a lot, but the time is wrong because I am still mourning.

However, I want you to know that I fear for your safety and am hoping to see you alive again. If you telegraph me that you are ready to nail them, I will be here as quickly as possible."

She nodded, feeling sad and confused but knew she could trust him to be at her side whenever she needed him. He got into the saddle and rode toward McDowry who had been waiting close by the cannons. As she watched them ride out of the fort's gate, she experienced a new emotion; she would miss the handsome Spaniard a great deal. She was confused by the feeling of losing more than the pleasure of a friend's company, but nevertheless, a small smile brightened her normally serious face.

"May God protect you, Armando Diaz and bring you back safely," she whispered as she turned around to bundle up her belongings in the cabin in preparation for her own departure.

CHAPTER TWELVE

* * *

THE PRIEST RODE BESIDE ARMANDO BUT REMAINED SILENT. HE DIDN'T DARE
ask the Spanish noble man how he felt as he seemed lost
in thought.

Armando's jawbones showed a tight line while he
reassured Ronan and himself over and over again that he
would see her alive in a few days. Yes, he would help her
bring justice down on the murderers of her father just as
she had helped him. "Even if I have to ride all the way to
hell for Elli Townsend, I will do it without a trace of fear
or hesitation," he told the priest.

* * *

Later that day Elli rode toward Jerome, another mining
boomtown not too far from Fort Whipple. She had dropped
the plan to go to Wickenburg after overhearing the conversation of two soldiers that three banditos robbed the bank
in Jerome. That sounded too much like Texas Logan to
ignore it. Elli hoped she was on the right track and could
still be in contact in Wickenburg or Prescott if the rumor
proved to be wrong.

Jerome was a thriving copper mining town with saloons and brothels. They even had a jail in the middle of Arizona Territory, so Elli hoped to find out new information.

When she arrived in Jerome she was surprised at the size of the town. She checked into the local hotel and rented a stall for Thunder. The hotel offered a chance for a bath, and she could even wash some of her clothes later that night. It was still early evening, and Elli had pampered herself with a juicy steak and baked potatoes at a restaurant called "Linda's Stove." The food was delicious and the prices reasonable. Elli felt like a new woman after the decent meal she had enjoyed.

Now she was on her way to one of the saloons in town. Streets were busy and some soiled doves tried to lure men into the houses of ill repute. It was loud, and the streets smelled of horse manure. Elli tried her best to camouflage the fact that she was attractive. Her hair was pinned up and hidden under the dusty cowboy hat and, as usual, she wore her father's shirt and riding pants. She had selected the biggest saloon from which loud piano music, laughter, and hollering drifted onto the main road. But she knew it wasn't completely safe for a woman to enter a saloon unless she was sporting girl of loose morals.

As Elli entered through the door, she found the place packed with people. It was noisy, and a young man playing a piano close to the bar had to pound his keys to be heard above the crowd. Cigar smoke hung thick in the air.

Heading toward the bartender, she took in most of the people while passing them. There was a game of faro going on at a table on the right side near the stairs.

At least two of the men looked like professional gamblers. Townsfolk and cowboys occupied a couple of tables, and local shady ladies sat on quite a few laps.

Elli noticed stairs leading up to chambers on the second floor where soiled doves must be practicing the oldest trade in the world. She was aware of the lustful looks of a few men and knew she had the appearance of a drifter. She didn't want to imagine what might be going through their minds about her.

Self-confident, she asked the bartender for a whiskey while her hand remained close to her father's holster. She felt safer while wearing the Peacemaker, and Elli knew how to use the gun. Her Pa had been a good teacher, preparing her to deal with any situation. In a place like this you never knew what a rowdy saddle tramp might do.

"Where do you come from, you pretty thing?" the bar dog asked. He had a big belly and rotten teeth. His eyes were small like a rat's. Elli instantly disliked him.

"Southwest from here, way east of Cochise County."

"What brings you all the way up here so alone?" The man was quite nosy.

"Just looking for some folks."

"Well, I would have use for a beautiful woman here. One of my painted cats got herself pregnant and can't work right now, if you know what I mean." He winked at her and slowly licked his lips. "Of course, we'd have to dress you a bit more appealing. Right now, you look like a tomboy."

Elli felt like smacking him in the face but stayed calm. Instead she lead the conversation in a different direction. "I heard you had a bank robbery not too long ago."

"Yeah, three members of a gang robbed the silver and gold exchange last month. Fortunately, most of it had been transferred to the bigger county bank just three days before the robbery. However, they shot the poor fellow on duty in a cold-blooded manner, even though he opened the safe for them. Must have been furious that most of the fortune was gone."

Elli opened her mouth and her eyes wide, pretending to be shocked. "Did they send a posse after them?" she asked.

The pimp was happy that he was able to fascinate this young woman with his stories, and bent toward her confidently. "Sure did, but they haven't been able to catch them yet. Texas Logan is way too smart for the law dogs."

"How do you know it was, what did you call him, 'Texas Logan'?"

"I saw them riding into town earlier, and he and the two Lenny brothers had a drink right here at this very bar where you're standing right now, young lady."

Elli emptied her shot of tongue oil and tipped her hat.

"Where are you going now, all alone, pretty little bird?" the bartender asked. "This is my saloon and you can stay as long as you wish. I'll make sure nobody bothers you."

She nodded and tossed a coin on the bar. "Thanks for the generous offer, but I just arrived, and I'm rather beat. It's been a long ride, I might consider your offer another day. But right now, it's time for me to hit the sack."

Elli Townsend played it diplomatically as the saloon owner seemed to be a willing source of gossip and information. When she turned and walked across the floor of the saloon, some guys whistled at her, and one grasped her wrist as she passed his poker table. "Stay here, little lady, you might be my lucky charm tonight."

Elli looked at him. With deadly steel in her voice and a smoldering stare in her eyes she turned toward him. "If you ever dare to touch me again, you'll see the end of this night much earlier than you wish."

He was ready to yank her onto his lap, but her cool posture and voice stopped him.

There was something about the woman that made him

nervous. "Might as well touch a rattlesnake!" he snarled to his friends. He let go of her and turned back to his game of poker.

Elli left the saloon. Some people stared after her, but nobody interfered with her brisk walk to the doors. She didn't see the grim looking cowboy with the dark beard get up from his place in a lonely corner. He left the saloon and watched her walk to the hotel. A few minutes later the same fellow entered the hotel as well. "Got any rooms for tonight?" he asked the man who ran the place with his wife.

"Just one but it doesn't include a bath. A young lady has paid for our hot water service already. I can handle only one in the copper tub per night."

"Yes, I saw her walking over from the saloon. Nice-looking if she dressed more like a woman, I'd say."

The owner of the hotel was just another man so he winked at the stranger and in a low whisper added, "Beautiful as sin. I peeked through the keyhole when she changed clothes and guess what? You wouldn't believe it. She's a sheriff's daughter and dares to walk alone into a saloon."

The stranger stared at him. "She's what?"

"A sheriff's daughter. I saw the badge on her nightstand, and asked the marshal here. He told me her name rang a bell, and that most likely that lady is the daughter of a Yuma County sheriff."

"Well, keep that room for me. I have something to take care of and will return in about two hours." He left the hotel through the main entrance in a hurry.

CHAPTER THIRTEEN

***

A LONE RIDER RODE THROUGH THE NIGHT. HE KNEW THE TRAIL WELL AND found the secluded log cabin right away. As he stopped his horse and jumped off, the cabin door flung open, and a man with a Winchester aiming at him yelled, "Hold it right there, hands up!"

"It's me, John. I have a message for Logan."

The fellow at the door waited until he could see the late visitor's face better in the shining light of a petroleum lamp on the porch.

"John, what brings you here so late? I hope nobody followed you."

The man who spoke stood next to the cowboy with the Winchester. "It's okay, Darrell, let him in."

John walked into the crude cabin and nodded his head at the third fellow sitting on a wooden bench. "Evening, Pete."

The leader turned away from the door to face John, staring at him with piercing eyes. "So, what brings you here?"

"There's a new woman in town."

"You must be kidding me. You ride all the way out here to tell me that?"

"She asked a lot of questions about the bank robbery. Actually, about the gang specifically." The guys frowned at this information and looked at each other nervously.

"Must be the bank guy's widow? Why else would she ask about that?"

John looked at them for a moment. "Actually, she's a sheriff's daughter."

All three outlaws started to laugh. Darrell was shaking with laughter as tears ran down his cheeks.

"Is she like a female deputy of some kind? Looks like the territory is short of law dogs."

"Believe it or not, that woman walked alone into the saloon. Doesn't seem to be part of a posse, but somehow she is searching for you guys."

The dark-haired man remained silent. Then he slowly turned toward the fireplace. The scar on his right cheek gave him a dangerous look. "A lawman's daughter looking for our company. Now that's something new. Well, why not turn the tables and enjoy playing a little game with her?" His slowly licked his lower lip.

CHAPTER FOURTEEN

***

ELLI ENJOYED THE STEAMING WATER IN THE COPPER TUB. HER BODY FELT TIRED, and for the first time since the morning at the fort, she allowed herself to think about Armando and Ronan McDowry. She hoped and prayed that they were okay. Armando's absence made her feel kind of lonely tonight. Elli had gotten used to the company of the Spanish rancher, not even realizing that he was becoming part of her heart.

The other thing that Elli Townsend wasn't aware of was that she had changed from being a hunter to being prey.

***

In a lonely log cabin out in the woods of Northern Arizona, a man lay awake while his two gang members were fast asleep and snoring loudly. The wakeful man had a dangerous glint in his eyes and a small smile curling his lips. "I'll see you soon, lawman's daughter," he whispered into the darkness. His lips parted into a cruel, wolfish smile.

***

Elli was alone in Jerome. Her companion Armando was on his way to Texas trying his best to protect the Irish priest Ronan McDowry and his gold statues.

She felt lonely on her hunt for Texas Logan and the dangerous Lenny brothers but, she was her father's daughter, and prepared herself to continue the chase until Armando's return. After all, she had been the one who had suggested they split up for a while, at least until McDowry got to Texas to board an eastbound train. Elli had no doubts at all that Armando would return to help her. He was a man of honor and, just like her, respected the law. Sheriff Townsend's daughter wouldn't rest until she saw the three men hanged. They deserved to die for murdering her beloved father and other men, too.

After hearing that the Logan gang had robbed the bank in Jerome, Elli decided to continue her search here. Who knows? She might be lucky enough to stumble across a trace of them. Her gut feeling told her that they were still hiding somewhere in the area. They could have never escaped a posse with their exhausted horses, and it would have been too risky for them to spend the bank's money too generously, too early, as it would awaken suspicion.

When she had talked to the intrusive bartender at the saloon the previous night, Elli hadn't realized that a man was observing her. The shady cowboy was obviously in contact with Texas Logan and the Lenny brothers. Little did Elli know that he had warned the entire gang, a dangerous development indeed, and with each passing hour the unavoidable confrontation came closer and closer, putting the beautiful woman in the highest danger.

Elli left town with early daylight and rode into the surrounding hills and canyons that sprawled around Jerome. The scenery was beautiful, but Elli had no eye for it. She was searching for tracks from Texas Logan and his compadres. Around noon she got off her horse Thunder and watered him at a shallow creek. So far, she hadn't found any signs at all but hadn't expected to be that lucky on the first day of her hunt. Elli kept her positive attitude while she filled her water flask.

Later that afternoon she rode into the small settlement of Sedona around thirty miles east of Jerome. Three houses, a cabin and a couple of barns and corrals were nestled among the breathtaking scenery. The farm was run by a farmer called Snebly along with his wife and family. A lovely river flanked by lush trees carved its way through several red rock canyons, creating natural water pools around the farm.

Seldom had Elli seen such a beautiful valley. *This is a true paradise,* she thought.

She was warmly welcomed by Mr. Snebly, and his wife invited her right away to have lunch with them. Elli accepted with a smile. The farmer was a rough looking guy, but he was as friendly as his wife. "I am William Snebly. What brings you into the isolation of our red rock country, ma'am?" He had a strong accent which Elli could not place.

"I am the daughter of the Yuma County Sheriff, way southwest from here. I'm on the tail of some outlaws."

Snebly's wife stared at her. A woman all by herself hunting men who broke the law! This was hard to believe. But then she remembered the gun holster around the visitor's slim hips. There was something about her that suggested she was a kind person, but one who wouldn't hesitate to use that gun.

Mrs. Snebly had been a hard-working farmer woman all her life. All she knew about the role of a female in the Wild West was to tend to the house and farm, the fields, and animals, and, of course, to raise the children.

The protection of all of that should be the work of the man. Mrs. Snebly didn't mention that to the strikingly pretty visitor in her kitchen.

As all family members were called to the huge wooden table inside the house, Mister Snebly let the topic drop for the time being.

His brother and three young kids stormed into the kitchen. The man stretched out his hand. "I am Hans Snebly, William's brother. Pleasure to meet you, ma'am."

Mrs. Snebly carried a huge pot with potatoes to the table. Fresh warm bread, a tray of baked ham, and garden greens followed.

"Oh my, that smells wonderful," Elli said while sniffing the mouthwatering aromas escaping the bowls.

Mrs. Snebly laughed. "Well, I didn't expect guests today, but I hope you enjoy it anyway."

The two younger kids, around six and nine years old, stared at the young woman. "Let us pray," said William Snebly while he folded his big hands. Everybody followed his example. "May God bless our day as we perform our given chores. Thank you, God, for granting us with a nice visitor today as well as the food prepared for us. Hold your protecting hand over her as well as over us. In Jesus's name we pray, Amen!"

"Amen!" everybody at the table answered.

Elli was deeply touched at being included in the prayer. It hadn't happened in a long time. But God knew she could use every prayer since it was uncertain if she would survive the mission she was on.

The food was excellent and, after a bit of awkward silence, everybody started to chat happily. Elli was painfully aware that she had no family left, no one to share her daily thoughts and worries with. She missed her father and her beloved mother more than ever at that particular moment. For a second, she thought about Armando, and wondered where he was right now, but then forced herself to stop thinking about his handsome features and black wavy hair.

One of the boys asked her, "Do you also run a farm, Lady?"

"Jeremy, do not bother her with your questions," interrupted his mother strictly.

Elli shook her head. "I work for the law, Jeremy, but maybe one day I might start a ranch and raise horses. And you may call me Elli."

The younger boy, Tom, as he had introduced himself, stared at her with unbelieving eyes. "You mean you are something like a sheriff?"

"No, Tom. My father was a sheriff. He encountered some bad fellers, and I am trying to finish his work by bringing them to justice." Elli had answered as cautiously as possible. She didn't want to scare the children.

"Are these men you look for dangerous? Do you have a gun, did you ever shoot anyone?" Tom was all excited.

"Tom, stop it!" Mister Snebly strict tone stopped his son from any further questioning.

"I don't mind him asking, but certain things are too upsetting for children to know. It's a rough world out there, and the longer they enjoy the sunny side of life, the better," explained Elli.

The children's mother smiled at her. This young lady seemed to have a sense for family after all.

When they finished their meal, Mrs. Snebly offered to make some coffee.

"I don't want to be a burden for you or interrupt your daily routine, Mrs. Snebly."

"Oh, please call me Anne," said the farmer's wife. "I

am so happy you came by. It doesn't happen very often that I get female company out here, Mrs.—?"

"Oh, just call me Elli!"

"Alright then, Elli! Does it stand for Eleanor?"

Elli smiled. "Eleonora, but everyone calls me Elli."

After finishing their coffee, the boys, their father, and uncle went back to continue working on the corrals.

The third child, a shy girl of perhaps seven years, stayed back to help her mother and Elli wash the dishes. Her name was Megan. She was a pretty blond girl with huge blue eyes and freckles around her nose.

She looked at Elli and smiled. "You look so pretty; do you have a daughter, too?"

Elli laughed. "No, honey, not yet. Maybe one day. But I think you are much, much prettier than me anyway."

Anne smiled at her daughter. It was easy to see that she was very proud of the little girl. Elli wondered if her own mother would be proud of her for what she was doing. Was she watching her from heaven? Was her mother worried or trying to protect her?

Once all the chores were done, Anne invited Elli to stay for the night, since it was late afternoon already.

"I don't want to cause you any extra work, Anne," Elli objected.

"You won't. It's so nice to have a woman here to talk to. It's beautiful in Sedona but also kind of lonely sometimes. I mean, I miss the company of another woman from time to time." Anne looked down at the floor as if to hide her loneliness.

Elli understood her too well. "I know what you mean, I don't have a family anymore. My parents are both dead, and I don't have any siblings either."

"Oh, that must be very lonely. No husband?"

Immediately Anne bit her tongue. She was embarrassed. She must appear so blunt. But Elli smiled at her.

"Not yet. I have some unfinished business on behalf of my late father I have to attend to first."

"You mentioned that he's dead. Those men that you're looking for, did they have something to do with his death?"

Elli looked at the elder woman, and the pain in her eyes touched Anne's heart and answered the question right away.

"They shot him, Anne. I'll not give up until I've brought justice upon them! They're nothing but cowards and have killed more than one man."

"I will pray for you that one day you'll be able to leave it all behind and that your heart shall be free of the sorrow the murder has created. I will pray and hope that you will find the sadness and anger replaced by the love of a caring man and a beautiful family."

"Thank you, Anne. I appreciate your words. But I can't stop this search until I take revenge for my Pa.

These outlaws robbed the only family I had, and I'll see them hang, even if it's the last thing I do."

Anne embraced her. She knew the woman had to battle her past and had to fight the men who had thrown her into this nightmare. Finally, she got up to show Elli her room for the night.

CHAPTER FIFTEEN

***

ELLI WALKED OUT OF THE HOUSE AND OFFERED TO HELP WITH FEEDING THE animals. The two Snebly men were thankful for extra hands, so they happily accepted.

"Do you have problems with road agents here?" Elli asked.

Anne's brother-in-law, Hans, shrugged. "Not really. We have a small tribe of Apaches in this area, but so far, they've been peaceful and friendly. We avoid them and they avoid us. Except for one warrior, he tends to come to our farm, and we trade furs and woven baskets with him. We pay them with corn crops and calico cloth for their women's clothes. He's really friendly and might be coming to the farm tomorrow. He shows up about every three weeks."

Elli was astonished to hear that, but then, on the other hand, why not? She had met only a few natives but had already learned that not all the bloodstained stories about Native Americans were true. There were indeed good and bad folks on either side of each race.

Dinner later that evening was simple yet tasty—freshly baked bread and cold cuts of the leftover ham and fresh cow milk. Elli enjoyed the company of the family a great deal and couldn't recall when she last had laughed so much.

Finally, she withdrew to the guest room to get some sleep, but felt lonely. Megan was very proud to offer her room to the pretty woman. Her brother Tom had said she was a real sheriff's daughter.

Elli said a prayer before she went to sleep and included the entire Snebly family as well as Armando and Ronan McDowry. She hoped both men were safe and close to Texas by now.

***

Beyond the border of Arizona in the middle of the New Mexico wilderness, the handsome Spanish rancher was staring up at the stars. McDowry, his snoring travel companion, was rolled up in his blanket next to the campfire. The handsome features of Armando Phillipe Diaz bore a sad expression. He was thinking of Elli, hoping and praying he would find her alive once he returned to Arizona. He told his Irish travel companion earlier that night that he couldn't help but worry. With a sigh Armando woke McDowry whose turn it was to take over the watch for the rest of the night. Armando hoped he would find some sleep for himself under the glittering stars of the cold night.

***

Elli had slept well and got up feeling refreshed. She went to the creek outside to wash her face and waved at the kids who were feeding the chickens. Anne had prepared biscuits and gravy. The coffee was strong and hot, just as Elli preferred. The two men sat at the table and were talking about building a new round pen.

"I wouldn't mind helping you. I'm used to hard work," Elli offered. After all, no one was waiting for her in Jerome, and she wanted to do something in return for the kind hospitality she had experienced from this family.

The Snebly brothers looked at each other and agreed they could indeed use every helping hand. The morning passed quickly, and the work was tough. It wasn't long before all were covered in dust and sweat, although the weather was much cooler here than in Yuma. Nevertheless, Elli enjoyed the company of the family members. They had a humble way of working together which showed their respect and gratitude for each other.

Unexpectedly, William Snebly turned around and waved a warm "hello." Elli looked for whom he was welcoming.

Next to the corral stood an Apache warrior, leading his horse with one hand and holding a rifle with the other.

The visitor greeted the brothers while staring at Elli. His face was friendly with the typical bronze Athabaskan features.

His long straight hair was held back by a red piece of cloth. He pointed at Hans. "You found a wife?"

Hans laughed. "No, Naiche. This is Elli Townsend. She's visiting us from the south."

Naiche came closer and looked at her. Elli greeted him pleasantly with a nod. The Apache carefully reached forward and touched a strand of her hair. "Apache hair. Dark as the night, but your skin is white like the moon." He was clearly astonished by the young woman. Then he looked at the men. "I brought beaver fur today and yucca ropes, but first before we trade, I will help you with the round corral."

Naiche's English was rough, but once Elli got used to it, she was able to understand him without difficulty. She liked the Apache immediately. It was obvious he was well respected among the whole Snebly family.

It reconfirmed what Elli had always assumed: It was

indeed possible to get along with Indians if everybody remained respectful.

When they were done, Anne and her daughter served them all homemade lemonade. Then Naiche showed them his goods, and they exchanged some sugar and dried beef as well as a beautifully woven saddle blanket for his extra help.

The children seemed to love Naiche, and he patiently explained everything to them. He played a song for them on a small bone flute . It was early evening when the Indian went back home to his small band of Northern Tonto Apaches. Anne invited Elli to stay one more night at the farmhouse, and she gladly accepted, since she was truly exhausted from the day's tough outdoor work.

The next morning, she planned to ride back to Jerome to catch up on the latest gossip going around town. She hoped to find out more about the current hiding place of Texas Logan and the two Lenny brothers. Hans and William decided to ride along as they had to get some goods for their farm at the local mercantile. Anne waved goodbye, and the children hugged their visitor for a farewell. William Snebly's wife was obviously sad because she had enjoyed Elli's company and hoped to see this wonderful lady alive again. After all Elli Townsend was on a very dangerous mission.

When Elli and the Snebly brothers rode into Jerome's Main Street, they witnessed a big turmoil at the end of the street. Men were shouting, and an obviously furious mob had gathered around a single person on a horse. People yelled at the man in the center, shaking their fists. The man's horse danced nervously.

"Good grief, that looks like a lynch mob right there," Elli remarked and pointed toward the scene.

Hans nodded. "I don't like it at all. What are they so upset about?"

"You should rather ask with whom are they so angry?" replied his brother William.

At that moment the group parted slightly and, to their shock, they saw Naiche on his frightened horse in the middle. The men tried to pull him off the animal's back, and the Apache was about to use his rifle. Elli kicked her heels into the flanks of her horse forcing him into a fast trot. "My God, they are about to lynch Naiche," she whispered. There were shouts of "thief" and "horse thief" and "hang him high."

"What's going on here?" Elli shouted but nobody paid any attention to her. Meanwhile, the two brothers caught up to the woman and tried to calm down the outraged people. Naiche looked straight at Elli.

A single shot ended the ruckus, and the men parted. Elli sat on her horse with a smoking pistol in her hand.

"The next one who lays a hand on this Apache will meet a bullet."

"This is none of your business, lady. He's just a lousy Apache who has stolen some stuff and probably even this horse," a rude looking town bully yelled.

"What makes you think he stole stuff, and if so, what is it that he's stolen?"

"Why would we explain it to you, woman? As I said before, stay out of it!"

Again, the mob started to draw closer around Naiche.

"I am here on behalf of Sheriff Townsend, and as an appointed deputy, I have the right to arrest you and to accompany this man into the safety of a sheriff's office until the problem is solved."

Some men laughed at her until she showed them her

badge and pointed her gun at the closest man who was trying to get hold of Naiche's rifle. "Whether you like it or not, step away from the man," she threatened. Meanwhile, the Snebly brothers had their barking irons aimed at the crowd, too. They were surprised by Elli's announcement.

This woman has some backbone coming up with a bluff like that, William thought. He was impressed.

Since this was about his friend Naiche, he would do anything to protect the man.

Obviously, Elli had the same opinion.

"I ask you once again, what did this man steal?"

"He stole the horse and the saddle blanket, as well. The horse holds a ranch brand. That's enough proof to hang him."

Suddenly Hans yelled at the crowd. "You're not going to hang anybody at all. This man has traded the horse and the saddle blanket on his visits to the Snebly farm in Sedona. I am Hans Snebly, and this Apache's name is Naiche. He's a friend of mine, whether you believe it or not. Naiche's done nothing wrong, and has always respected my property and that of my brother William here as well. You have my word and that of the sheriff's deputy from Yuma. This lady was with us when we gave him the saddle blanket as a gift yesterday. Let go of this man immediately or, I swear to God, you will regret it!"

The people around Naiche stared at the Snebly party, their anger still boiling. It was obvious they were all hungry for a necktie party.

But they were also aware of the three loaded guns pointing straight at them at close range, and none of them were willing to risk their own life for a little hanging fun. Slowly, one after the other they turned around and walked away from the scene.

"Are you okay, Naiche"? Elli asked.

He nodded. "I thank you, white woman with Apache hair. You are a brave and strong warrior. You saved me. I shall never forget that."

Hans and William escorted Naiche to the mercantile and promised to ride back with him as soon as they had gathered everything.

"Be careful now, Elli Townsend, you might have just made yourself some enemies by messing up their entertainment," Hans said. They shook hands. "My family's farm is always a place you can call home. In case we hear something about those outlaws, we'll let you know somehow. If you need help, you know where to find us."

Elli took their hands, thankful to have won new friends. She knew chances were, she would need them someday when it was time to encounter the three murderers.

CHAPTER SIXTEEN

***

NO ONE PAID ATTENTION TO THE MAN STANDING AT THE CORNER OF THE SALOON watching the whole scene. He'd been wondering where that Yuma sheriff's daughter had been the past three days when he hadn't seen her around town.

You're quite a tough and brave little lady, riding against an angry mob to save a redskin, he thought. He knew that Texas Logan would enjoy his dirty little hunting game against that beautiful, yet so daring, female. John would never get in Texas Logan's way, but, *dang, was that woman tempting,* he thought.

***

Meanwhile, Texas Logan looked at the two Lenny brothers as Darrell asked, "Why don't we just go somewhere else, boss?"

"I think Pete's right, Logan. Let's just get out of here, and spend the bank money with some hot Mexican señoritas," Darrell laughed.

"What in the world is wrong with you guys? Are you scared of a silly woman who wants to play law dog and outlaw? Besides, have you forgotten that we didn't get as much actual out of Jerome's bank as expected? We stay in this area. End of discussion!"

Logan looked at his two gang members. It was obvious they didn't like it, but they'd never dare to speak up against him. In one way, he was right. One sheriff or deputy or posse member, more or less, chasing them wouldn't make much difference. And both of them agreed that even the thought of a woman hunting them down was ridiculous anyway.

Texas Logan looked at them. "Well, I tell you what, John spilled some interesting news the other night when he told us about that wannabe deputy woman. We might be able to catch an even bigger fish than the Jerome bank savings."

Now Pete and Darrell were all ears. Their leader motioned them to the table in their hideout shack, and poured himself some of the bitter coffee.

"John happens to know that the monthly payment of the cavalry based at Fort Whipple will be very a tempting target this time as they're expecting some extra expenses for new buildings and weapons. The talk is of gold, money, and a couple of new kinds of rifle with ammunition as well. An escorted wagon is due to bring the load to the fort. But since nobody is supposed to know about it, the escort won't be very big, only a handful of soldiers, I figure. They don't want to draw too much attention, I reckon."

Pete scratched his stubbly chin. "How come John knows about it then? I mean, how trustworthy is that spark?"

Darrell nodded in agreement to his brother's doubts. Logan looked at them.

"Let's put it this way, he's charmed himself into the bed of one of the officers' wives. The little bird has sung a sweet melody about this wagon being expected and said he might get a new rifle as a gift for his Prince Charming qualities."

Both brothers laughed. Yes, John was definitely a lady hunter. "He'll ride with us, and we'll give him a twenty percent share. There's still more than enough for us, and that way we can keep an eye on him to make sure he doesn't stab us in the back. Besides, it won't hurt to have an additional gun at hand."

Darrell got up and poured some coffee into a battered tin cup. "When is the transport supposed to be in this area?"

"John said the captain at the fort has received a telegraph; the wagon is on its way already and expected east of Fort Whipple in about five days from now. They'll pass through a small canyon on the way. That'll be the ideal spot to ambush them. The escape route leads us right into New Mexico and from there to Mexico to your hot señoritas, Darrell. Meanwhile, we might enjoy a little game with that wannabe posse woman."

Logan was smiling, but it was an ice-cold smile that didn't touch his slanty eyes—those eyes that gave chills to every decent man who respected the law.

***

Elli was back in The Jerome Hotel. The town had remained quiet despite the nasty scene in the afternoon. The Snebly brothers and Naiche left as quickly as possible. They didn't want to take any chances. The townspeople might get nasty again after a few too many shots of bottled courage at the local saloons.

The next morning, she walked over to the restaurant and ordered a hearty breakfast. Elli had gone back to the hotel without eating dinner the previous evening, and she was starving. But she didn't take unnecessary risks in the dark and had been too shaken by the fact that Naiche had encountered such unexpected life-threatening situation only one day after they met.

While eating breakfast in the restaurant, a stranger walked up to her. He took off his hat and smiled. "Ma'am, may I introduce myself? My name is John Harker. I've come to know that you're looking for a certain fellow named Texas Logan. Is that true?"

She eyed him suspiciously. Uneasy about his unexpected approach, she nodded. "Eleonora Townsend. Who told you so?"

"I happened to overhear your conversation with the bartender the other day. Please pardon me for addressing you so bluntly, but I might have some information that could be helpful in your search."

"Why would you want to help me?" Elli didn't mean to be rude but there was something about this fellow that she disliked, or at least distrusted, right from the first minute. Her late father had called it a sheriff's gut feeling. He had always told her that if she was a real woman of the law, she would be able to smell outlaws even five miles away against the wind. The thought of her Pa caused her to smile.

John Harker misunderstood that as an invitation to sit down at her table. He had always been self-confident when it came to his effect on women. This one was a particularly pretty one, he had to admit. Elli didn't deny him the seat as she had made up her mind to listen to his story. *Who knows? It might be really helpful.*

"So what information are you talking about?"

Damn, this woman is really tempting, John mused. He looked at her and said "Well, I heard that Texas Logan rides through the Payson area from time to time. Rumors have it that he plans to steal some cattle there."

"Who told you so? Why should you know what he plans, and where he will strike?"

Now Elli's eyes had turned into slits. *Yes, this guy actually didn't only smell of outlaw, he literally stank like a skunk.* She didn't trust him worth a nickel.

"Do you happen to know which ranch he intends to steal the cattle from, by any chance?" she asked him sweetly.

"I overheard two shady guys the other day at the saloon. They're known for riding with Logan from time to time, and they mentioned the Nichols Ranch close by Camp Verde. I'm pretty sure they were referring to Logan's plans."

Elli stared at her coffee mug, remaining silent. John was confused. It seemed like this lady didn't believe him as easily as other women did. That was a new experience. She started to resemble prey to him, but he wouldn't try to charm her any further. Logan had his own plans for her and John wouldn get in the way. If he did, he'd be a dead man.

"It seems you overhear a lot in that saloon, mister." He didn't miss the sarcastic tone in her voice.

"Well, I thought it was my duty to let you know since you're the daughter of a lawman like people told me, and our sheriff here doesn't seem like someone to ride the river with. He wasn't even able to protect our money in the bank. I was truly impressed how you saved that Apache's life yesterday, and I thought you might be the right person to save that poor rancher's cattle out there, too. The cattle rustling is supposed to take place in two days as far as I've understood. I'm certain the brand artists are supposed to find buyers who wouldn't question the brand."

Elli looked at the man named John. It sounded like a true story. However, she couldn't ignore her doubts.

"Well, I'd better get going. Business is waiting. It was a pleasure talking with you, ma'am." He got up, turned, and walked away from the table.

I wonder what kind of business you are really after, mis-ter, Elli thought. She watched the people at the other tables as John Harker left. None of the guests greeted him or paid any attention. Another hint that Elli's gut feeling about that man was right. He wasn't liked among the townspeople, either that or not known to the locals. Unfortunately, Elli didn't know which one it was.

* * *

Sheriff Townsend's daughter tried to find out more about the Nichols Ranch by asking folks around town, but no one knew the place.

She went to the post office and sent a telegram to a Texas fort where Armando was supposed to drop off the Irish priest with his precious gold statues. From there, Mc-Dowry was supposed to take the train to the East Coast. She informed Armando that she was following a new lead and was now based in Jerome.

Elli wanted to make sure that Armando knew where to find her so that he wouldn't ride to Wickenburg by mistake. After all, that was the town where he would expect her to be if not updated. She surely missed him, but would, of course, never admit that. So she only added a simple line to the telegram that she hoped all was going well for them and signed it "Eleonora Townsend."

After that was done, Elli went over to the mercantile and bought a few items to make sure she had enough food for an overnight stay in the wilderness. After all, she might not find the Nichols Ranch right away. The rest of the day she remained in town to keep eyes and ears open for further information. The cattle rustling was to take place in another two days according to that Harker fellow.

Elli saw a small church at the end of a side alley. Her intuition urged her to walk over to it.

As she entered the small building her father's gun holster around her hip seemed to weigh double what it usually did. It felt wrong to wear the gun into a church. Elli slowly walked toward the altar. The smell of candle wax and flowers lingered in the air.

It was a peaceful, quiet place. Sunlight streamed through the stained glass windows and scattered into thousands of colored dots on the opposite wall. Elli went down on her knees and prayed. She prayed for her father's soul and her Mom, prayed for the safety of Armando and Ronan, and for the Snebly family who had been so friendly to her. She also prayed for Naiche's safety and freedom, and was aware that the natives were in constant danger of being troubled by the white man.

Finally, Elli sat in one of the plain wooden benches and enjoyed the silence and special atmosphere of the church. She was nervous but couldn't name the reason for it. Somehow, she had the feeling that she was closer to Texas Logan than thought. He seemed like a ghost, always a step ahead of her but always present in some corner of her mind. She couldn't recall a single day or night that she hadn't thought of the murderers since that fateful day when she had hugged her dead father on the dusty main street of Yuma. Would there ever be peace for her again?

Witnessing Armando's grief that was still present even after his wife's murderers were hanged, it was doubtful.

And then, what if she achieved her final revenge? What would happen in her life after that? Would Elli stay in Yuma? Would Armando disappear out of her life just the way he had appeared so unexpectedly?

Would he vanish just the way her parents had? Elli was

aware that she had no one left in her life and it brought her to tears. For the first time the woman was scared of the future. Elli had always been a serious young lady, but today she faced a new form of melancholia totally unknown to her. She forced herself to leave the church and shake off the unpleasant thoughts. She planned to depart for Camp Verde by early next morning. Unfortunately, the location of the Nichols Ranch was still unknown to her.

CHAPTER SEVENTEEN

***

ELLI SADDLED THUNDER WITH THE FIRST DAYLIGHT AND RODE OUT OF TOWN.
Opposite the stable, one of the curtains of the brothel moved
slightly as John Harker watched her riding away.

"Well, well, wonder if you don't ride toward Camp
Verde, little lady," he whispered.

"What did you say, darling?"

He turned around to the blond calico queen in his bed.
He couldn't even remember her name. She had been a
temporary amusement while his thoughts had returned to
the black-haired Elli Townsend more than once.

That woman was surely a true challenge for every man,
he thought. He got dressed and threw some coins on the
bed for the prostitute without even looking at her—that
soiled dove didn't matter to him at all.

***

Elli rode toward the east. It should take her at least four to
five hours to get to the Camp Verde area. The country was
pretty. Pine trees lined her route and a lot of deer greeted
her on the way.

She enjoyed the clear, crisp morning air. It was much cooler up here than in her hometown. She stopped at a creek from time to time for a drink of the cool water and to take a bite from her food supplies. Around noon Elli reached the small town of Camp Verde where she asked the people about the Nichols Ranch. Most folks shrugged their shoulders. It seemed that no one knew the place. Finally, she ran into an old guy in front of the local barber shop.

"Excuse me, sir, how do I get to the Nichols Ranch?"

He looked at her and then pointed east. "About an hour's ride from here, ma'am. Nothing much around there, though."

"What do you mean?" Elli asked.

"I don't know if they're still running that place. The old man died some time ago. A snake got the best of him; he lost his leg and got the fever. After that I've not seen any of the family in town."

"Thanks for your help, sir. Where can I get a decent meal around here?"

"Down the street, Old Betty's is our restaurant. Nothing fancy but the pies are really good."

She thanked the man and headed toward the place.

He was right, the pies were really delicious and Elli ate two pieces with three glasses of homemade lemonade.

She asked about the Nichols place again, but no one could tell her if the ranch was still being operated or not.

This is strange, thought Elli.

However, according to the old guy, the ranch really did exist. That much of John Harker's story proved to be true. So far, so good.

She decided it was too late in the afternoon already and didn't want to risk getting lost in unknown terrain in the dark. So, she paid for an extra box in the livery stable and made up her mind to spend the night next to her horse sleeping in the straw. She didn't mind it at all but loved the homey smell of hay and horses and found their sounds comforting. She used her saddle as head rest and a wool blanket to keep herself warm.

***

Hundreds of miles east, Armando lay awake. He and his Irish protégé had arrived safely at the fort in Texas and the priest was lucky as he was able to join an escort of high-ranking officers back to the East Coast.

McDowry had told Armando that he felt safe enough to travel with them, and that his Spanish friend should try to make it back to Elli as quickly as possible. The Irish was as worried about her safety as Armando was.

Ronan would never forget what Elli and the Spaniard had done for him and couldn't help but fear the worst for the young lady.

Now Armando held Elli's telegram in his hand which he had received upon arrival at the fort. She was in Jerome now, and he felt uneasy about the "new information" Elli had mentioned in the short note. Somehow, she seemed to be getting too close to Texas Logan and the Lenny brothers. That crazy stubborn sheriff's daughter that had saved him. The fellow hoped he could be at her side in time because there was no doubt that she would need him urgently once she found the pack.

Armando smiled when he thought of her, but during the past few hours, a strange, heavy feeling had spread throughout his chest. Instead of being happy to receive the telegram it left him more nervous than ever since leaving her behind at the fort. McDowry had to hold him back from jumping onto his horse and riding right back to Arizona.

Armando needed to rest and make sure that the man of the Good Book got safely onto this train along with the military guys.

As the Spaniard tried to find some sleep, the Irish priest watched him tossing and turning with nightmares most likely not only about his murdered wife but also of the beautiful Elli Townsend. The Irishman kept praying for Elli.

Early the next morning Ronan forced Armando to at least eat a decent breakfast and took the opportunity to sincerely thank his loyal friend once again. When the train was about to depart from the location, the two men shook hands.

"Please make sure she is safe, Armando," McDowry whispered. "You might not have overcome your lost love yet, but one day you and Elli might share more than the hunt for those killers. You'd better make sure she is still alive when that moment comes."

"Thank you, Ronan, I will see to that! Who knows? I might even visit you in Ireland if I should ever set foot in my Spanish homeland again."

Armando knew the priest was very fond of Elli. After all, it had been she who had helped him find the lost treasure of his ancestor.

"I will send a letter to Yuma when I reach Irish shores. May God bless you both my friend and may He protect you. I will always owe you my very life."

Armando nodded. Then he watched the Irishman get into the train car. He waved through the window and was glad to see that at least twenty-five soldiers would be accompanying the train to the East Coast.

He waved again as the steam from the locomotive erupted in one immense hissing cloud and the shrieking whistle announced the departure of the train.

"May God protect you and the four evangelists, too," whispered Armando.

Only a few minutes later the people in the fort spotted a dark-haired man on his horse riding through the main gate. He took off as if the devil himself were after him. The devil wasn't after him, but after a woman in Arizona who meant more to him than his stubborn mind would admit. But his heart knew too well that Armando Phillipe Diaz was on his way to that woman, and he hoped and prayed that he wasn't too late.

CHAPTER EIGHTEEN

***

ELLI LEFT THE LIVERY STABLE AT FIRST DAYLIGHT. SHE WAS ON HER WAY TO find the home of the Nichols family. Today was the day the cattle rustling should happen. It took her over two hours, but finally she saw the ranch building hidden in the woods. The gate displayed the initials so she knew she found the right property and approached the place carefully. Strangely, the ranch looked abandoned just as the old barber in town had predicted. Elli got off her horse and looked around. There was no sign of people or cattle. She called out. "Hello, Mister Nichols?" No answer.

Something's wrong here. Elli pulled her pistol from its holster and walked around the house. The corrals were empty, no trace of livestock at all. Was she too late? Had Texas Logan's gang already stolen everything they had been able to lay their hands on? Where was the Nichols family?

Elli turned around and watched Thunder growing more and more nervous with each passing second. Something seemed weird, but she couldn't pin it down. It bothered her, so she walked toward the house and knocked at the door. No one answered.

The sheriff's daughter opened the door and saw a thick layer of dust on the ground. Apparently, no one had been in this building for a long time.

Probably that John in Jerome understood a wrong name when he had overheard the conversation in the saloon, she mused and walked outside again. Suddenly it struck her what had disturbed her ever since she had arrived at the ranch. The birds ... there were so many trees, but not a single sound, not a single bird was chirping. Elli cocked the hammer of her pistol. She knew she was in trouble.

***

Armando rode like Sam Hill himself, but he could not risk killing his horse. He knew it would take him at least five days of hard riding with only a few hours of sleep to return to the Jerome area. Five days under these circumstances seemed like an eternity to him. The priest had convinced him that once he hit the trail, his nervousness would cease, but the opposite was the case. He became more anxious with each passing hour. The handsome rancher hardly took any breaks, except for watering his horse, letting it rest for an hour, and eating a few bites from his well-stocked saddlebag. It was evening now, and the sun was setting in gorgeous colors.

Armando had to find a place to camp and give his exhausted horse a much-needed break.

Another four days, he thought. Four days that could decide the fate of Elli for good or bad. The tired man sensed that something wasn't right. He couldn't name it, but his gut feeling grew stronger and stronger. He'd always been able to trust his gut.

***

Elli listened closely but heard nothing. Slowly she turned in a circle. The shadows had grown longer with the late afternoon sun in the west. She felt as if she were being watched before she heard the click of a gun. The thundering sound of a rifle being shot off echoed in the woods. Elli didn't have a chance to react.

* * *

Armando Phillipe Diaz failed to find any rest; he tossed and turned next to the campfire, trying not to panic as the feeling that he was too late held his heart in an icy grip. He had no explanation for the chills running up and down his spine. When he finally fell into a shallow slumber, Elli's face haunted his dreams.

* * *

She heard the sound of the gunshot, but all she felt was being knocked off her feet, and a heavy weight slamming into her chest. Her body flew backward a few feet.

As she fell, Elli saw her horse pull back so hard that the reins loosened from her hand. The stallion bolted and fled the ranch in panic. "Thunder," she whispered. Then the world turned dark.

* * *

Armando took a sip from his flask before walking to his horse. He got into the saddle with a bite of beef jerky between his grim lips. The nervous feeling hadn't disappeared overnight. Being an excellent rider, the man tried to make as many miles as the condition of his horse would allow.

Armando left the Texas territory behind, and was about to cross into New Mexico. As he came into the next town, he bought a second, much stronger horse and didn't mind the expense. He still had his ranch in Orange Grove and was well off. This way Armando would at least be able to switch horses and could cover more ground without killing the poor animals. The urge to reach Elli as fast as possible was almost unbearable.

***

Elli woke up. She felt the hard ground under her hips, and a burning pain in her upper chest. She smelled the iron scent of her own blood and knew she had been shot. Her vision was blurry, and she slumped on the floor of the Nichols ranch house. A man sat opposite aiming a gun at her.

"Hey Logan, I think your little deputy bird is waking up," the man with the six-shooter chuckled. Elli was too weakened by the numbing pain to turn her head toward the voice.

She heard boots walking toward her. A fellow stared down at her, his eyes glittering with excitement and his lips curled into a cruel smile.

"Well, well, well, lady. I hope you slept well. That shotgun kind of blew your lights out for a while, and we had to wait for you to wake up to play with us."

Elli shook her head, tried hard to concentrate, and to clear her vision. The man came closer and stared into her pretty face.

It was clear that she was badly wounded. He could see the sweat forming on her forehead. Nevertheless, she aroused Logan. John had been right; she was a pretty thing.

"Did you really think you could catch Texas Logan and the Lenny brothers with that pistol of your dead father's? You walked right into our trap didn't you, little girl?"

So, this was Texas Logan. Finally, she met the murderer

of her beloved Pa. But she was helpless and knew she had been hit hard, her strength vanishing. Her arm was numb, and she started to feel cold.

This was bad, really bad, and Elli knew it. She was mad at herself and should have known better. After all, it had sounded fishy right from the start. Elli Townsend knew she was about to die.

CHAPTER NINETEEN

***

ARMANDO WAS SWEATING AND EXHAUSTED LIKE NEVER BEFORE IN HIS ENTIRE life. Elli's friend had ridden the whole day and now it was late at night. Another two days and he would be in Jerome. He knew he needed rest if he wanted to make it, and so did his two horses. It had been a good idea to get a second horse. Armando had made more miles than expected just as he had hoped when he bought the second mare.

The tired rancher tried to eat some beans that he'd cooked over his campfire but wasn't really hungry. Armando had no explanation for the feeling but he sensed that something was wrong. The man stared at the sky, a full moon red like blood added to his discomfort. "Blood moon, oh God, don't let that be an omen," he whispered and started to pray.

***

Elli stared at the killer she had been looking for since she had left Yuma. It seemed like ages ago. Texas Logan gazed back at her, and so did another unidentified guy. The third gang member was nowhere to be seen. Logan bent down, and his hand lifted her chin.

"A beautiful lawman's daughter you are. I might as well have some fun with you before I kill you!"

She looked at him, her eyes furious small slits. She spit right into his face.

"My name is Elli, Miss Elli Townsend, you rotten piece of crap!" she hissed at him. Her hatred took him by surprise, and the man next to him caught his breath. Texas Logan hit her hard in the face. Elli felt her lip split, and she tasted blood, but she didn't care.

The hate sent waves of adrenalin through her body. She had no other wish than to kill this man, right here, right now, even if it was the last thing she ever did. Elli would kill him with her bare hands if she got the chance.

Logan got up. He jerked her up on her feet. She winced as the pain in her chest made her feel faint. Logan pulled her across the room, then threw her onto an old bunk bed. "I'll teach you a lesson not to spit on me!" he growled as he slowly walked toward her, opening his belt.

That moment the front door flew open with a loud crash. "Pete, Logan, they're coming!" Darrell came running into the house, rifle in hand. His face was pale, and he obviously was scared to death.

"Wait outside until I'm done with her, Darrell," Texas Logan yelled back at him.

"No, we need to get out of here, they're coming!"

"What are you talking about?"

Darrell had stopped his panicked approach and turned around to his brother. Pete was still aiming his six shooter at Elli, but she was barely aware of it. She had lost a lot of blood; it was still soaking her blouse and she felt sleepy and dizzy.

"Redskins. There's a whole band of them, and they're

surrounding the house. Looks like they've come for us."

"Indians? You must be kidding me. What Indians?"

"From the looks of 'em, I'd say Apaches. I have no idea what they're doing here, but they're watching the house," Darrell explained.

Pete had walked over to the window and carefully peeked out. As he did so, a rifle shot hit the frame of the window, splitting the wood. Logan cursed and ducked away immediately. So did Pete.

"How many of them, Darrell?" Texas Logan yelled.

"At least fifteen. We have no chance."

Logan looked around. He knew their horses were behind the ranch building in the corral, if the Apaches hadn't gotten to them already. "The back door, quick, it's our only chance to get out of here," he whispered.

He and the Lenny brothers retreated slowly toward the door. "What about her?" Pete asked pointing at Elli. She was pale and lay shaking on the bunk bed.

"Never mind, she's going to die one way or the other. Just a shame I missed my fun with her." Texas Logan left the building through the back door, not once glancing at wounded Elli Townsend.

The Apaches followed the fleeing outlaws as they escaped on horseback. Darrell cried out in pain when an arrow hit him in the right thigh. They rode for their survival kicking their horses hard.

Elli was nearly lifeless on the bunk, the sounds of fighting, horses and gunshots echoing in her ears. She felt cold and sweaty and her strength was dwindling fast. The pale woman knew she would be killed, but it didn't matter anymore. When Elli heard the sound of someone walking toward her, she forced her eyes open. The face was blurry at first, then it became clearer. The Apache lifted her carefully and carried her out of the house.

"Naiche," she whispered and then fell into deep blackness.

* * *

Armando woke toward dawn when the night reached its darkest right before the sun welcomed a new day.

His heart was pounding, and he was fully awake. Awake with fear and the feeling of certainty that he was too late. There wasn't anything more he could do. He sat for a minute not moving at all—his heart felt heavy. Then Armando remembered his father's voice telling him, "Son, you will never be worthy in God's eyes if you give up too early. Only He has the right to decide when it is too late and when it isn't, when you succeed or when you won't."

With a deep sigh he stood up and washed himself in the creek behind last night's camp. As he combed back his long black hair with his fingers, he looked at the rising sun setting the sky on fire while the water covered his bare muscular shoulders. The sky was red. *Red like blood,* he mused and tried hard to shake off the unpleasant memories of the pools of blood around his dying wife, an image he would most likely never forget.

CHAPTER TWENTY

***

DARKNESS, COMFORTING ETERNAL DARKNESS. THE DRUMMING SOUND OF A single heart beating, weak and shallow. Boom, boom, boom. Shadows of canyons flying by, the shriek of an eagle as it soared high above in the sky, closer and closer to the sun. As she looked into the sun, the light almost blinded her eyes. Pain, so much pain. Again, the beat of the drum. Boom, boom, boom. The pain and the fever raging through her like a wild river, tearing her apart. Time and faces flying by behind her closed eyes. Then heat and again the terrible pain in her chest getting worse, making her body jerk.

"Will she survive?" a calm voice whispered.

Another answered. "Only if it is meant to be by the Great Spirit. The fever is her biggest enemy right now. It has to leave her body, and will I try to heal her with all that the Great Spirit has taught me, but she lost too much blood. You might have been too late when you saved her from those white eyes. She is young and strong but is more on the dark side of the world and almost with her ancestors right now. However, she was meant to meet you. I saw you and her riding together in a vision. Usen, our creator, never sends visions without a meaning.

"Cleanse yourself in a sweat lodge and fast and pray for her. You may send her your spirit animal to lead her out of the Valley of Darkness."

Naiche nodded at the tribe's medicine man. He had known him since childhood days, and he knew his medicine was strong. He would obey his instructions. If the white warrior woman was supposed to survive, then Naiche would do whatever it took to help his medicine man try to save her. After all, he owed the woman his own life.

Their spiritual leader named Kaywaykla looked at him. "I have to remove that bullet or the fever will kill her. It might kill her if I do so, anyway. You will have to hold her. The bullet is very close to the lung, but I have no choice."

Naiche looked at him and nodded. Like everybody in his band, he trusted Kaywaykla completely. He spoke with the spirits and knew every plant and prayer ceremony and had saved many of them. He was gifted by Usen, the Apache creator of the world, who was so sadly disrespected by the white eyes, as they called the foreign intruders.

The spiritual leader of the tribe had removed the white woman's blouse. He looked at her. She was beautiful. But he didn't feel attracted to her in an erotic way.

The medicine man had seen her in a vision weeks ago, and so he hadn't been surprised when Naiche had told the story about the woman saving him the other day in Jerome. Kaywaykla knew they were meant to ride together one day, and he had also been the person who saw her in acute danger. The man could speak to his ancestors and the spirits around them. He had sent Naiche to look for her as he and his warriors were excellent trackers, like all Apaches, and it hadn't taken him long to find out where she was. But when

Naiche arrived, it had been too late, and she had been shot by the outlaws already.

Kaywaykla started singing the holy songs of the creator while he cleansed both their bodies with the smoke from sage collected earlier at a secret place. He stuck a knife in the fire pit under the brush shelter where they had placed her, allowing the fire to cleanse it.

The small group of Tonto Apaches all tried their best to help Naiche and Kaywaykla to save the white woman warrior with Apache hair. The medicine man finally took the knife, let it cool for a moment, and motioned to Naiche to hold her shoulders tight. The warrior placed his hands on her body and signaled that he was ready. Her skin felt damp and hot.

"Please, Usen, lead my hand and protect this woman," the old Apache prayed. Then he carefully cut the wound, slowly searching for the lead bullet.

Elli moaned in her fever-stricken dreams. Finally, he found the metal in the heavily bleeding wound. As the tip of the knife dug under the bullet, Elli opened her eyes, and a scream of pain escaped her lips. She stared right into Naiche's eyes hovering above her pale sweaty face, then her vision went black again and all she felt were pain waves crashing through her body, making it jerk. As Kaywaykla pulled out the knife with the bullet, a spurt of blood followed.

More blood that she loses, Naiche thought and he swallowed hard. He doubted that she would survive this, but he knew their spiritual leader had no other choice. The lead bullet had started to poison the remaining blood in the young woman's body since it had entered her torso.

***

Armando rode hard, crossing the Arizona border. He tried to shake off the feeling of hopelessness and to remain positive. But what if she had found Texas Logan and the Lenny brothers? What if she had gone after them without waiting for him? He shook his head as if to force the thoughts out of his troubled mind. She had promised to wait, but he also knew that, if he were in her shoes and found the murderers, he would not have waited a single day himself.

Nothing would stop her if she had the chance to lay hands on the killers. Who wouldn't understand that, especially Armando?

***

Darkness, complete darkness. A floating sensation. Then a movement. A brown shadow moving slowly, carefully, staring at her. The eyes like gleaming coals. Sharp teeth and a deep growling sound. Time flying by, the mountain lion gazing at her, then turning around walking away, turning its head looking back at her. Should she follow? Darkness again, and the sound of her heart, a steady vibrating boom, boom, boom.

Naiche played the drum in harmony with his own heartbeat. The leather pouch with the mountain lion's teeth rising and falling on his naked chest with each deep breath he took. The cougar, also known as a mountain lion, was his spirit animal. He sent it down into the darkness where Elli was trapped, battling the fever and battling the wings of death, death that was trying to keep her for eternity. Naiche knew his warriors protected the small camp well. Often the younger ones criticized him for being friendly with the Snebly family, but he knew it was their only chance to survive. Too many Apaches had been deported already, sent away to an unknown country. Naiche tried to live peacefully for the sake of protecting his family and his band.

Nobody on the Snebly farm had the slightest idea that their Apache friend was the leader and chief of his small tribe and was well-respected among the entire Apache nation.

Boom, boom, boom. Her heart beat rapidly along with the rhythm of Naiche's drum.

The mountain lion looked at her again, waiting patiently while Elli drifted further down into the choking darkness, not feeling her body any longer. And she didn't feel the pain either, just peace. Boom, boom, boom. The drum went on throughout the entire night and far beyond the hours of dawn.

CHAPTER TWENTY-ONE

***

FINALLY, ARIZONA! ANOTHER DAY TO JEROME. ARMANDO COULDN'T RECALL ever having felt so dragged out in his entire life. He had spent the night at a small cavalry outpost and had been thankful for the company of the men. He appeared filthy, unshaved, and unwashed, wearing dirty clothes, and he had gratefully accepted the offered barber set and a fresh shirt. When the Spaniard saw his reflection in the shaving mirror, he gasped. He barely recognized himself. The face in the mirror was thinner, and a dark beard emphasized his ghostly appearance. His black hair had grown and hung into his face in wild curls. His clothes looked shabby. The eyes were restless and clouded with worry for Elli Townsend's safety.

Armando washed and shaved and felt a bit better. He bought some extra rations of oats from the soldiers for his two horses. So far, they had been strong and loyal animals, true companions on a backbreaking ride of long days and short nights. He decided to keep both of them once this trip to hell was over. "Thunder would probably approve of that idea," he chuckled.

With a smile he thought of Elli's magnificent stallion.

He asked if there was any news from the Jerome area, but nobody at the outpost knew much except that the bank had been robbed and a man shot. However, the soldiers told Armando about a wagon with gold and rifles that had been stolen two days ago not far from their camp, and that the escort had been ambushed and killed in a canyon half a day's ride from here.

As Armando looked up into the night's sky, he saw the full moon and, just like the previous night, it was an eerie, red blood moon that seemed to follow the Spaniard's desperate ride against time.

The troop was scheduled to leave the outpost the next day. Their mission was to find the pack of road agents that had robbed the military transport and murdered their fellow soldiers. Armando was still nervous. He got the feeling that this holdup had something to do with Texas Logan and the rotten Lenny brothers. He left the camp along with the cavalry at first daylight. While they rode southeast toward the canyon where their fellow soldiers had been massacred, Armando chose the route west toward Jerome and the Arizona upper country.

***

The mountain lion watched her, waiting while a low growl escaped his mouth. Then he turned around and slowly walked a few steps, waiting for Elli's spirit to follow.

She stared back at him and finally took a small step toward the magnificent animal, then another one, and another step. Slowly the cougar and the sound of her heart as it echoed the drum beat lead her out of the eternal darkness that had surrounded her for days.

Naiche sat there, his eyes closed while he communicated with his spirit animal. He was exhausted and hadn't slept the past three days and, if not for Kaywaykla's tea with spirit plants he would have collapsed by now. His eyes were bloodshot and he felt dizzy, but his hand continued to beat the drum in its slow rhythm. The steady sound symbolizing their creator's heartbeat had echoed through the camp since the tribe's spiritual leader removed the bullet from the young woman's chest.

The old medicine man softly touched Chief Naiche's shoulder and watched him open his tired eyes. The younger Apache looked at him and saw him smile. Kaywaykla pointed toward the dark-haired woman. Naiche turned his head and saw that her eyes were open. He carefully touched her face; the fever had gone down. She was still in danger but Naiche knew that her chances to escape the darkness of death were much better now.

For the first time since he had picked her body up at the Nichols Ranch there was a spark of hope that she would make it. Only now Naiche would allow himself to eat something and sleep a few hours. He handed over the drum and care for his white friend to Kaywaykla and his wife. He felt dragged out but content doing so.

* * *

Armando arrived in Jerome late at night. His legs were weak and his two horses were covered in sweat. He walked into the rental stable and made sure both animals were rubbed down, watered, and fed well. Then he paid the owner some extra coins and laid down in the straw next to the horse boxes. The Spaniard wanted so much to check on Elli right away, but he finally had to give in to his fatigue and slept as if unconscious. At least Armando was in Jerome and hoped he would see her alive in a few hours.

The next morning, Armando went over to the hotel, and

asked for Elli Townsend. The owner of the hotel looked at him suspiciously. "She had a room here, paid four days in advance, and then disappeared on the second day.

Well, I won't return the two days she paid for nothing because I held her room after all," the guy shrugged his shoulders as if to excuse his greediness.

"Any idea where she went?" Armando asked. He was deeply troubled by her disappearance.

"No, I reckon it is the way folks are. I mean, first, she disappeared, and then another guy who booked a room the same day left, too. But unlike your friend Miss Townsend, that feller even forgot to pay. I hope the sheriff here arrests him when they find that scum."

Armando thanked the man and went for breakfast before he searched for her. The restaurant was a busy place. He ordered some bacon and eggs and ate hungrily as it was his first decent meal in many days. *My God, where do I start looking for her?*

When the lady who ran the restaurant came over with a refill of strong, steaming coffee, he asked her about Elli Townsend. Armando described her and wanted to know if the lady had seen her.

"Oh yes, who could forget her? She cuts a figure with her looks despite the clothes and holster she wears. Yes, she was here, had my famous pancake breakfast," the woman declared with a wide grin.

"When was that?" Armando asked.

"Four days ago, I'd say, haven't seen her since then, though. She must have left town after she met that shady fellow," the restaurant owner guessed.

"What shady fellow?" Armando asked alarmed.

The elder lady looked at him carefully and Armando sensed her discomfort. "I'm a close friend, and we were supposed to meet here."

That seemed to reassure her enough to talk. "This fellow is in town from time to time. He's a crook, nobody likes him. He'd been seen with shady people in the past, if you know what I mean. However, that scum started talking to your friend the morning she ate here, but I don't know what they spoke about. Only thing I'm sure about is, that your friend didn't seem to like him much either. Her posturing was clear. That flannel mouth disappeared shortly after your friend Elli left town and has not been seen the past two or three days. The day after he spoke to Elli, I met to one of the saloon girls. I feed them a free meal from time to time. No need to look down on the fallen angels, right?"

Armando looked at her in astonishment. A woman that fed ladies of the night for free was rare but spoke volumes for her generous heart. He instantly liked her for that.

Unlike other men, he had never been tempted to use the services of a soiled dove but also had never looked down on them.

"Well, Margie came here all angry about that guy who had spent the night with her. She said he had been brutal and rude and had watched that dark-haired Townsend woman leave town next morning. He had seemed more interested in her than in Margie."

"What did he say about my friend?" Armando was on high alert now.

"Something like that he was wondering if she rode toward Camp Verde. I'm sorry, that's all I know."

Armando thanked her and paid, leaving a generous tip, rose and decided to ride to Camp Verde right away. The urge to find Elli was overwhelming now. He didn't like the story about that crook at all. And why had that shady character left town right after Elli?

CHAPTER TWENTY-TWO

* * *

AS SOON AS THE WOUNDED WOMAN WOKE FROM UNCONSCIOUSNESS, THE stabbing pain returned with full force. Her chest was on fire and her left arm felt numb. She had no idea where she was, but she knew that Apache people were around her, taking care of her. Slowly the memories came back.

The face of Texas Logan. The Nichols Ranch. The gunshot that had thrown her off her feet. Her worst enemy threatening her. The sudden appearance of Naiche and his warriors. How in the world did he get there in time? How did Naiche know where to find her? Suddenly, a thought struck her mind. "Thunder," she called out and tried to get up but cried out in pain and her vision grew blurry.

Kaywaykla held her back. "Your horse is safe, caught by Naiche's brother. The stallion is with us. You must rest."

Elli looked at the old man. "Thank you," she whispered as she sank back on the fur covered ground. An Apache woman appeared, smiling shyly as she offered her some stew. Elli was too weak to eat so the woman fed her slowly with a wooden spoon. Then she lay back and almost immediately fell asleep.

***

Armando arrived in Camp Verde four hours after he left
Jerome. His mare regained energy after the night's rest and
extra oats, and he covered the distance faster than expected.
Armando asked around and hoped somebody could tell him
about Elli's whereabouts. No one seemed to know where
she was, but some people remembered her asking for the
Nichols Ranch. Armando headed out of town following the
directions they gave. He found the ranch thanks to the fresh
tracks. Behind some pine trees he saw the ranch building,
but it was obviously abandoned.

*If nobody lives here anymore, why in the world are there
so many tracks?* He was confused about it. The Spaniard
knew right away that something was wrong and slowly
pulled his rifle out of its scabbard while he rode toward
the ranch house. It was very quiet and he didn't like the
isolated location of the place.

In front of the house Armando counted dozens of boot
prints as well as the flat prints of moccasins. Sure as a
gun something was wrong here so he held tight to his
Winchester, ready to fire it at any time. There was no
sound, neither of cattle, nor people. Armando cautiously
sneaked toward the door then saw the bullet hole in the
window frame.

From the color of the chipped wood it was obviously a
fresh mark. Armando was certain that something terrible
must have happened here, then slowly opened the door and
took a careful step into the house.

***

"You saved me, Naiche," the white woman whispered. She
was still very weak, but now it was certain that she would
survive the shotgun wound.

"I just returned what you have done for me, white warrior with Apache hair."

She smiled at her title. "I saw you there in the darkness. You were the cougar, weren't you? But how is that possible?"

"Never question the Great Creator's ways and the power of your spirit animal; the eagle is your totem. Strong medicine."

"How did you know I was there at the Nichols Ranch. How did you find me?"

"Kaywaykla, our medicine man, saw you in a vision. He knew you were the woman who saved me in Jerome. We never doubt his visions, he talks to the Great Spirit, and is a holy man."

Elli nodded. The sound of a horse coming closer distracted her. As she peered out of the sheltered wickiup she saw a young Apache leading Thunder toward them.

The horse nickered when she spotted her owner, and tears of joy filled Elli's eyes. "Thunder," she whispered. The stallion bent his head and carefully sniffed at her hair, snorting happily into the mass of black waves. It made her laugh, and although that hurt her chest wound, she felt alive and much better.

***

Armando felt sick to his stomach. The terrible day at his ranch in Orange Grove when he found his dying wife seemed to repeat itself. The house was empty, but the simple, rural furniture was overthrown, the room a chaotic mess. It was obvious there had been a fight. The back door stood wide open, and dirty boot tracks traces lead out of that door.

He called Elli's name. No answer. As the confused

Spaniard turned around, he stared at the ground in disbelief. It was almost as if a cruel twist of destiny had brought him back to his own personal nightmare. There was a big puddle of dried blood on the floor and on the old, dirty bunkbed on the other side of the cabin he saw even more blood.

Armando stared at the stain trying to control his panic. *Calm down, amigo, you do not even know if she has been here. You heard the stories of outlaws in the area, it could be anybody's blood.*

He chanted the sentence again and again to comfort himself.

He read the tracks that lay in abundance inside and outside the house. Obviously, white men had been in the house as he could read from the footprints on the dusty ranch floor. From the many moccasin prints in front of the house, he guessed that the Indians attacked.

Strange, he thought. According to what he knew about the tribes in this area, they would rather wipe out their tracks, unless they had been in a hurry to continue their hunt or to leave the place.

When the Spanish nobleman walked to the back side of the ranch house, he saw that three horses had taken off from there. There had been horses with horseshoes and some Indian ponies following them, but only for a short distance. He found a trace of dried blood on a branch, but not enough to suggest that it had been the wounded person from inside the house. Whoever suffered a wound losing that much blood on the hardwood floor was surely mortally wounded.

Armando was devastated. He still had no clue where Elli Townsend was.

Just as he was tempted to think that she hadn't been in this cabin but likely ended up somewhere else or back in

Jerome, all of his hopes shattered like a breaking glass. He spotted it, but his heart didn't want to believe what he saw. Armando stared at the dirty hardwood floor. Slowly he bent down and picked up an item.

The scream of a man resounded through the woods. The scream was barely human, but more like a wounded animal.

The devastated man stared down at his hand holding the sheriff's badge between his shaking fingers. The engraved words, "Yuma Territory," were barely readable under the dried blood covered the badge. He staggered out of the ranch home blinded by tears. Now there was proof that she had been in the house and he knew … he was certain … that it was her blood on the floor. Too much blood. Armando's heart sank. His hope to see her again was gone. Her body was missing, but he swore to himself that he would find her. He needed to bury her. Gently the handsome man pushed the sheriff's badge into his vest pocket. Despite its tin material, it weighed as heavy as his guilt about not protecting his beautiful friend.

He jumped into the saddle and took off from the ranch and the blood stains in the house. Over and over the same question in his mind: Where was Elli Townsend's body?

Armando arrived late at night in Jerome and rented a room at the local hotel. He felt devastated, cold, and hopeless.

"Any luck finding that pretty lady?" the owner asked. Armando shook his head.

The expression on the Spaniard's face stopped the hotel owner from bothering him with further questions. "Sir, my wife cooked some stew and green beans, also baked some bread. If you wish, I can send some up to your room. You look as if you could use some rest."

Armando nodded gratefully. He could not bear the

thought of having to face people and wasn't really hungry anyway.

Only a few minutes later the hotel owner's wife knocked at his door and handed him a plate of warm food. Armando thanked her and quickly closed the door again. He hadn't felt hungry before, but as he took the first bite, he realized that he hadn't eaten since morning and his body finally gave in to his need for food and rest. While he chewed, his thoughts returned to the Nichols Ranch in Camp Verde.

Armando hadn't touched the sheriff's badge since finding it. He didn't have the heart to look at it right now.

After he finished his meal and a cat wash at the bowl with the pitcher of cold water on the table, the exhausted man took off his clothes and lay on the bed. Despite the loud music from the saloon across the street he fell asleep the moment his head touched the pillow. He was bothered by nightmares of a dark-haired woman dying alone while she called out for him to save her.

CHAPTER TWENTY-THREE

***

ARMANDO FELT TERRIBLE WHEN HE GOT UP THE NEXT MORNING. HE LEFT THE hotel in a grouchy mood and walked over to the restaurant. The place was busy, but Armando found a quiet corner and ordered extra strong coffee and a ranch breakfast. While he sipped on his first cup, the owner walked over with a plate of appetizing smelling scrambled eggs with crispy bacon. She served him wearing a warm smile. After all, even with a stubbly beard and dark circles under his eyes he still looked like a gentleman of the first water.

"What brings you to town, Cowboy? Wait a minute; I remember seeing your handsome face before. Any luck finding your pretty lady friend?" she cheerfully asked him.

"Not yet. She didn't show up here again, did she?" he asked hopefully.

She gave him a puzzled look. "No, she hasn't returned to the restaurant since she left and if the lady was back in town, I would know it, believe me. This place is better than any newspaper. All information and news gathers here, so to speak." To emphasize her words, she pointed at the crowd sitting around the different tables. It was quite noisy in the restaurant.

Armando's face turned into a mask of grief. The restaurant owner sensed his distress, and despite the busy time of the day sat with him for a few minutes. She waved her kitchen help to tend to the guests for a while, then poured herself a cup of coffee and refilled the man's cup too. He stared at the steaming beverage.

"Okay, what's the matter, Cowboy?"

"Call me Armando, if you don't mind. I found evidence that Elli might be hurt or even worse and hope and pray that I'm wrong. I really need to find her. She helped me in a very dangerous situation and saved my life."

The lady looked at him. "You love her, don't you?"

Armando shook his head. "I just lost my wife a few months ago."

"Well, your eyes show the same kind of pain now that you think you lost this Yuma sheriff's daughter. You may be able to fool yourself, but you can't hide love from an old hen like me. Believe me; I know love when I see it, and you do love that woman. Actually, I kind of took a liking to her at first sight. She's an ace-high person. Let me think about the facts we know, and then we'll come up with a plan to search for her."

The Spanish rancher smiled at the woman sitting next to him. He was surely glad he had come to this place this morning. Somehow this lady was so positive, she gave him hope that there might be a chance that Elli was still alive despite the discouraging facts.

"First of all, call me Frieda and finish your food. You can't think without a decent meal in your belly."

She watched him while he chewed, and only after he had dutifully emptied the whole plate did she start to talk.

"Well, your friend came into town and she was immediately the center of attention."

Armando looked at Frieda, a puzzled expression on his face. "Why is that?"

"That day we had an ugly crowd on Main Street. They were out on a little lynching party trail. Tried to kill an Apache called Naiche for stealing stuff, which he didn't, by the way. Elli Townsend had just arrived in town with the Snebly brothers."

"Wait, Snebly brothers? Who are they?" Armando wanted to know everything.

"They run a ranch in Sedona. Elli must have met them, and it looks like she made friends with them. I think it's easy for her to make friends," she added with a smile.

Armando reconfirmed that with a nod.

"When the mob was about to hang poor Naiche, Elli rode straight into the angry group of men, saving him. The two Sneblys supported her but, it was three guns against the whole furious mob. She didn't seem to be scared at all."

Armando couldn't help but mumble, "Dio' mio, you crazy woman," under his breath but he also felt proud of her.

"If you asked me, I would try to get in touch with the two brothers from Sedona and maybe even with Naiche. Those Apaches are incredible trackers, and if she is still somewhere out there, they will help you find her."

Armando thought about it. "I think you're right, Frieda. That's good advice. I thank you. How much do I owe you for the meal?"

She brushed the question off. "You are more than welcome. Not many decent men around here lately. I'm glad I could help you, so you are my guest today."

"Well, I'd better get going, ma'am."

Frieda nodded and after giving him the directions to

Sedona, she waved him goodbye. "God, I pray you find her alive," she whispered as she watched him leave the restaurant.

A few minutes later Armando was on his way to Sedona and the Snebly ranch.

He barely saw the beautiful country around him and tried not to have high hopes. But he wouldn't give up on Elli until he saw her dead body with his own eyes. So far, the Spanish rancher had no idea how he should face that moment when it came and feared the heartbreaking pain.

When Armando arrived in the red rock canyons around Sedona he was surprised by the immense beauty of the area. Never before had he seen such rich red colored rock formations in contrast with the lush green trees and the blue of the early afternoon sky. *What a place to run a ranch,* he mused while he slowed down his mare.

Finally, Armando arrived in the small settlement and rode toward the main ranch building. Two men building a new stable saw the stranger getting off his horse.

CHAPTER TWENTY-FOUR

***

NAICHE CAREFULLY HELPED ELLI STAND. SHE FELT WEAK AND DIZZY AND HE had to support her to make sure she didn't fall. According to the medicine man, she should be strong enough now to take a short walk. She had lost the sense of time and days and it was important to get her moving so she could become stronger again.

Elli had no idea how long she had been in Naiche's camp but knew she must have been unconscious for days, and her recovery was very slow.

Medicine man Kaywaykla had wrapped some kind of bandaging around her wounded torso. It was filled with herbs and was supposed to help her wound heal faster. By now the white woman trusted the wisdom of the old man. After all, he had brought her back to life from an nearly fatal gunshot wound.

The first few steps and deep breaths hurt like hell, but it helped raise her low blood pressure. Naiche remained at her side. They walked toward a small creek. "If you feel like washing yourself, I will send my wife to you. She can help to wash your hair and body, but be careful not to get the bandage wet and keep the wound covered."

"I would really like to wash myself a bit. I feel filthy after the days under the wickiup shelter and the fever. I also need to wash my blouse."

Naiche looked at the blouse and saw the hole where the bullet had entered. *How close she had been to dying.*

The Apache chief helped her sit on a rock next to the shallow creek and asked her to wait a minute. Elli tried to soak up the warmth of the sun when Naiche's wife, a pretty Apache female walked up. The woman nodded and after placing a bundle she carried next to the rock, Naiche's wife helped Elli slowly wade into the cool stream. She carefully undressed the white woman and softly touched the bandage. She knew that Elli had been closer to death than life the past few days.

Her husband said that the white woman was a great female warrior, and Naiche's wife was thankful that Elli had saved her husband from the angry mob in Jerome. She rubbed down Elli's skin with sage and a rough yucca plant sponge, and used a hollow gourd to scoop fresh water over her black hair. The Apache woman was careful not to move the herbal dressing over Elli's chest. Then she motioned Elli to return to the rock where she could sit down, and the white woman was glad she could do so. Her legs were trembling. Elli felt refreshed but exhausted and a bit shaky.

Naiche's wife tapped her own chest and said, "My name is Dah Des Te. I thank you for saving my husband, Naiche. You are a member of our family now." With those simple words she started to comb out Elli's wet hair with a bone comb.

The wounded woman was touched by Dah Des Te's words. "I have to speak to your husband." Dah Des Te nodded.

But when Elli wanted to reach for her blouse, Naiche's wife shook her head and handed her a wonderful hand sewn blouse of dark blue cotton. "Too much bad medicine in your old clothes." The apache woman helped Elli pull the blue cotton top carefully over her head, then smiled at her. "My gift to you, white woman with Apache hair." She also slipped a pretty necklace made from seeds and dried mesquite beans over Elli's head.

Elli touched the cheek of the Apache woman softly. "I thank you, Dah Des Te."

"We will burn your blouse now. Too much spirit of the dark side in it," the Apache whispered. Elli agreed. Then she slowly walked back to the camp. Naiche's wife remained at her side until she placed Elli safely under the brush shelter. There, her friend and Kaywaykla were waiting for her. They both knew that the talk the white warrior woman had in mind was going to be very serious.

***

Armando tipped his hat and greeted the two farmers pleasantly. "Excuse me, gentlemen, but I'm looking for the Snebly brothers."

"That would be us. What can we do for you, sir?"

"My name is Armando Phillipe Diaz. I came here because I need your help."

Hans looked at the stranger. "What kind of help?"

Armando wrapped the reins of his horse around a post on the fence next to him. William Snebly watched him. The Spaniard took his hat off and pushed strands of his long black hair back. He turned his hat in his hands nervously.

"I am searching for a friend of mine, Elli Townsend. The folks in Jerome told me you met her before."

William watched Armando carefully. After all, they knew that her father had encountered trouble with some outlaws, and the two brothers had never seen this dark-haired stranger before.

"Yes, we know Elli Townsend. What do you want from her"? Hans asked suspiciously. They were uncertain about the intentions of this Spanish-looking buckaroo.

"I believe she is in great danger if not worse, and I really need to find her," Armando explained. He couldn't hide the fear in his voice.

That moment Anne Snebly walked out on the porch. She observed the handsome visitor.

Armando greeted her. "Ma'am," and nodded with a friendly smile.

"Hans, what is it?" Anne wanted to know.

Her brother-in-law pointed toward the Spanish fellow and his horse. "This gentleman claims to know Elli Townsend, and that she is in danger. His name is Diaz something," Hans added rudely. The two men were very protective about their new friend, Elli. But Anne had turned pale.

"Oh, my God, you are Armando, aren't you?"

Armando nodded.

"She told me about you. Hans, William, he's the gentleman Elli saved in California after people murdered his family. She told me all about it when she spilled the beans about being on the hunt for those outlaws. Forgive us, Mr. Diaz; we are not used to lots of unknown visitors out here."

Ignoring the surprised faces of her husband and her brother-in-law, Anne took Armando's arm and invited him into the house. The brothers both shrugged their shoulders in astonishment and followed her as well. Anne served Armando cool water from the pitcher and prepared a pot of fresh coffee.

All four sat down at the table and listened to Armando's story about how Elli had saved him, and how they achieved justice for his murdered family. Then he explained that they had split up for a few days, but of course he didn't mention finding the gold statues. When Armando reached the point about the Nichols Ranch and all the blood he had seen there, Anne clapped her hands in front of her face whispering "No, dear God, no."

The man from California felt that Elli had made true friends here in a very short time and admired her deeply for that.

"What is your plan now, Mister—?"

"Call me Armando, please." He looked at William who had spoken first.

"Okay, then, Armando. What do you want to do now?" William repeated his question. It was easy to see that he and his brother Hans were very worried about the whole story.

"I haven't found her body yet. I need to, even if only to bury her. I owe her my life, and not just that, she gave my family the chance to rest peacefully as she found the true murderers. But she even might be badly wounded and still alive. As long as I haven't seen her dead body, I refuse to accept her death, although the amount of blood I saw spoke a clear language."

Anne's eyes were filled with tears. Meanwhile her children had walked into the house but remained quiet in the kitchen, sensing that something terrible must have happened to the nice lady who had visited a few days ago.

"We understand and will try to help you. One of us has to remain with the ranch and the family here, but the other will accompany you," Hans suggested while he poured his guest a cup of steaming coffee.

William nodded, and then turned toward Hans. "I reckon you plan to ride with him?"

There was no arguing about it. Armando admired the respectful way this family communicated. It was obvious they shared great love for each other. It reminded him of his late parents and the way they had brought him up.

"I want you to stay here tonight and eat with us. You can sleep in one of the boy's rooms," Anne insisted.

Armando agreed because it made it easier for them to start their search for Elli with the early morning light. While having dinner, William suggested they should ride to the camp of Naiche's tribe first.

"They are excellent trackers and he will surely help us. She saved his life in Jerome."

"I heard that story. She tends to take big risks, but I sure am glad she was able to save your friend."

The men decided that Hans and Armando would ride to Naiche's camp in the early morning and try to get the Apaches to help them in their search for Elli.

When Armando went to sleep in the older son's room, he thought about the Snebly family. It was easy to see why Elli must have liked them right from the start. Thoughts about her and about his dead family back in Orange Grove crossed his mind and it hurt. Like many times during the past months he asked himself aloud "What crime have I committed to be punished like that by destiny? Why do I have to lose everyone who is close to me?"

Again, and again, he cursed himself for leaving the stubborn Yuma woman alone for the sake of protecting that Irish priest with his gold statues. Armando felt miserable. He hadn't been able to protect his late wife and her parents and now had failed to protect Elli as well who had done so much for him.

With a sad sigh Armando rolled over and tried to get some sleep. He didn't want to think about what he might encounter once they found Elli. There was no way he could get himself to face the fact that most probably he would find Elli's decaying body somewhere out there.

CHAPTER TWENTY-FIVE

***

NAICHE AND KAYWAYKLA REGARDED HER. "WE UNDERSTAND THAT YOU WISH to hunt down those men who shot you and who killed your father. But don't do it until you are prepared and don't consider following them without the help of friends riding by your side," Naiche declared as the medicine man nodded.

"Once you feel stronger, our chief here will accompany you. It is a matter of honor. Like his wife said, you are family now, and we help and protect each other." Kaywaykla's words warmed her heart, yet she disagreed.

"I won't allow Naiche to get himself into danger because of me," Elli argued. "His tribe needs him, and I would never forgive myself if something happened to him."

Naiche laughed. "I am an Apache. We are always in danger as you witnessed in Jerome."

***

Hans and Armando left the ranch in Sedona with the first rays of sun warming the magnificent red rocks around them. They were both worried and prepared for the worst. Despite a spark of hope, both knew the chances were almost zero of finding Elli alive.

While they rode to the camp of the Tonto Apaches, Hans told Armando about the unusual friendship and trading partnership between his family and the tribe. Armando liked the man even more for the respect shown to the Native Americans. After all, the Spaniard was from a different cultural background as well, which hadn't made it easier to settle in a new country.

He told Hans how Elli had ridden to his ranch looking for evidence of the murder, and how she had put herself into danger by calling out the corrupt judge to trick him into confessing his crime. Hans was impressed but not at all surprised and knew that Elli was a valiant woman. He had witnessed it when she rode right into the center of the angry men in Jerome.

Armando Diaz reflected on his deeper feelings for the young, pretty woman. He couldn't allow himself to feel that way, so soon after the death of his wife. No, what he felt for Elli was friendship and loyalty … so far.

***

Naiche and Kaywaykla interrupted their conversation with the white woman when their scout came running to the wickiup shelter where they sat. "Two white men are coming on horseback, one with hair as dark as the night. The other looks like your friend Snebly."

Naiche nodded and jumped to his feet. He wondered what his white friend wanted here. He hardly ever visited the camp.

When the two men rode into the village, Apaches immediately surrounded them. Armando felt a bit uneasy. After all, the Apaches were said to be the bravest and deadliest fighters among the native tribes. Naiche and Hans exchanged friendly words, greeting each other like long-lost friends. Armando got off his horse and watched the scene in respectful silence.

Suddenly the circle of Apaches opened for a frail looking woman who slowly walked toward him. She wore a lovely blue calico blouse, and her black hair hung loosely over her shoulder. Her complexion was ashen, and her hollow cheeks added to her ghostly appearance. Armando had to squint against the glaring sun to see her at all.

At last, he realized that the woman wasn't an Apache but the missing Elli Townsend. He cried out in disbelief and dropped the reins of his horse, stumbling toward her. The surprised man gathered her into his arms, but she cried out in pain. Armando stepped back and saw the bandage strapped on her shoulder, and how pale and thin she appeared. He realized that she was badly injured and hugged her more carefully.

"I thought you were dead, God forgive me, but I thought I would never see you again," he whispered into her hair.

"How did you get here, how did you know where to find me?" Elli asked, confused. She was so happy to see him, she could barely speak.

Naiche watched the scene and smiled. "Come and sit with me. Hans and your friend William can follow us, too," he suggested as he pointed toward the brush shelter. A small boy took the horses to the creek to water them, and Dah Des Te offered them some water from a gourd bottle.

***

Armando couldn't take his eyes off Elli. He could hardly believe that she was alive. It seemed like a miracle to him.

Never had he expected this day to take such a lucky turn. But when he studied the dark circles under her eyes and her unsteady gait to the shelter, he understood that she must have been in very serious condition. His heart broke for her.

Armando and the others sat next to her under the shady roof of branches. "I tried to return as quickly as possible, but I was too late. I felt so guilty when I found the scene of carnage at the Nichols Ranch."

She smiled at him. "Is McDowry safe?"

Armando laughed. *Typical Elli Townsend. More worried about others than herself.*

"He made it safely onto the train to the East Coast with a whole group of military men at his side to protect him. He is as safe as one can be in this country."

Elli was glad to hear that. "How did you find me?"

He explained how he had heard about her going to Camp Verde, how he rode out to the ranch, discovered it was abandoned, saw all the blood, and was sure she was dead.

She looked at him with huge eyes, even paler than before. "How did you know it was my blood?"

Armando reached into his pocket. He carefully pulled out the blood-stained sheriff's badge and gently put it into her hand. She stared at it. When she looked into his eyes, tears rolled down her cheeks. He gently wiped them away.

Kaywaykla watched at her and then regarded the white men. "Let's take a walk to the fire and smoke the pipe together. Woman with Apache hair should rest now," he ordered strictly.

Elli wanted to argue against it, but she was too exhausted to move. Her Spanish friend rose after reassuring her that he wouldn't leave camp without her. She smiled weakly and closed her eyes. It hurt Armando to see her so frail.

As the men walked to the village's main campfire where the other warriors waited, Armando turned toward Naiche. "How bad is she wounded?"

"We always speak the truth even if it is a painful one. She was on the dark side of the world for many days. If not for our Kaywaykla's medicine, we would have lost her. She is still too weak to ride but still wants to follow those cowards who shot her down while they hid in the bushes waiting for her as if she was their prey."

Armando trembled with rage hearing that. Kaywaykla touched his arm. "Calm down. Only a fool would let love or hate lead his actions. We have to make a plan. Naiche will ride with you and the white warrior woman once she is strong enough."

Hans had followed the conversation. "You'd better include me. She's also my friend. We will ride at her side and finish off those bastards, once and for all. When they tried to ambush her so cowardly, they were three against one ... but next time it will be four against three. They'd better prepare themselves to have their last stand soon. This area has suffered long enough from robberies and killings committed by Texas Logan and the Lenny brothers."

They spoke for a long time that evening while the stars glittered above them. Hans and Armando decided to remain at the campfire among their Apache friends. The Spanish rancher couldn't put into words how relieved he was that Elli was alive and safe.

My God, how close he had been to losing her! He swore to himself never to leave her side again until they had found and shot or hanged those banditos. Armando was sure that she wouldn't be lucky enough to survive a second time if she encountered them alone again. He looked over at the warrior named Naiche and knew he would be

this man's friend for the rest of his life. He was grateful
that the Apache chief had searched for Elli just because
the medicine man had a vision about her being in danger.
Armando didn't know many white men who would have
done the same for a woman. Yes, he truly was grateful
and swore to himself to always have the Apache's back,
no matter what.

CHAPTER TWENTY-SIX

* * *

EARLY THE NEXT MORNING HANS RODE BACK TO THE RANCH IN SEDONA TO TELL his family the latest news. He knew they must be worried, especially Anne, who was very fond of Elli. Hans told the others that he would return in five days to ride with them on their vendetta against Texas Logan and the Lenny brothers under the condition Elli Townsend was strong enough by then.

* * *

Armando went hunting and fishing with Naiche and a few members of the tribe. He felt very much at ease with the Apaches and learned more about them and their way of life. As he learned their philosophy and beliefs, he came to understand that the cruelty white people blamed them for was self-defense in their daily struggle to keep their traditions alive. All they wanted was to live the way they had for centuries. Naiche was friendly and patient as he taught Armando the red man's way of fishing and hunting. They felt almost like brothers.

***

Elli grew stronger and stronger with each passing day. She spent a lot of time with Naiche's wife, Dah Des Te. She enjoyed the woman's company and watched her cooking. She learned how to make flat bread from mesquite flour and the way the Apaches prepared squash.

Kaywaykla checked on her wound from time to time, and after another three days he was able to remove the bandage. Elli looked at the old medicine man. "Thank you for saving me. I will never forget that. From now on I'll not only protect the white man's law but also my Apache friends."

He nodded and smiled at her. "You already did when you saved Naiche's life in that ruthless mining town. He is our chief. The band would have been lost without him. Naiche is a wise leader."

"You are an incredible medicine man, Kaywaykla. You healed me when I was almost dead. And you can see the future."

"The future looks dark and sad for the Apaches just like the black sky on a summer storm. I am old, but one day all of us will be lost. I have seen it in my visions many times. I hope I can at least save Naiche's family somehow."

"If I can help you with that, I will, I swear," Elli touched her chest over heart as she spoke.

Kaywaykla nodded. "I know you will, and I am glad the Great Spirit, whom we call Usen, sent you to cross our paths. Now let's go and see if that man from across the big water had any luck fishing."

Elli laughed at Armando's nickname. She knew that he was well-liked among the tribal members and it had dawned on her how happy she had been to see him riding into camp. He had kept his promise to return. What had touched her even more was how thankful and relieved he had been to see her alive.

*　*　*

Meanwhile, Hans had arrived back at his ranch and prepared himself for the hunt against the Texas Logan gang. Anne had been relieved to hear that Elli Townsend was alive and safe, but she cried hard when she heard how close she had been to dying from an almost fatal gunshot. William and Hans both knew that Anne had grown very fond of Elli, and they both hoped that the charming Yuma woman would visit them once in a while when this madness was over.

William was worried about Hans joining the vendetta ride but also knew they would never be at peace in this entire area as long as outlaws like Texas Logan or the Lenny brothers were alive.

They were a danger to their families and cattle as well as to their money in the bank. It was high time for law and justice to settle that gang's hash.

William knew he had to stay back with his family but helped Hans pack for the long ride and added an extra gun and bullets when they saddled his horse. When it was time for Hans to ride back into Naiche's camp, William hugged him hard. "You'd better make sure you return safely, brother. I need you here at the ranch and I need you as a brother even more!" Hans nodded, a lump in his throat as he hugged his niece and nephews and Anne.

His sister-in-law handed him a small necklace with a golden cross pendant. "Please, give this to Elli. She should wear it while on that revenge mission. It was given to me by my mother and always protected me well. She can bring it back once that business is settled, and when I can enclose her in my arms like the sister I never had."

Anne wiped away the tears and placed the necklace carefully into her brother-in-law's hand. He and William were deeply touched by this and realized how much Anne liked the late sheriff's daughter.

Then the younger Snebly brother mounted and rode off with a last gentle wave to them.

He truly loved his brother and the entire family and was worried about leaving them behind. He hoped and prayed that he would see them again alive.

It was late afternoon when Hans rode into the camp of the Apaches. The scouts had announced him early on. The tribe was well protected and the Sedona farmer was happy to see how well Elli was doing.

They spoke about the planned vendetta around the campfire later that evening. Armando told them about the robbery of the military wagon, and the approximate location where it had happened. He was sure that the Logan gang had committed the hold up.

***

"I assume they went down to Mexico. They mentioned Mexican women and tequila," Elli said.

By now she felt strong enough to ride. Together they studied the map, and together, they all decided to start their search on the route south to the Mexican territory.

Elli was eager to track the curly wolves. But now her wish for revenge was more controlled. It had changed from rageful anger to ice-cold determination. She would see them hang. She would make sure they ended up as dead as door nails.

Armando felt the same urge to kill those cowards. He

was madder than a hornet at the thought that they had laid hands on her.

The next sunrise painted the sky in glorious Arizona colors, setting it on fire.

Kaywaykla blessed Naiche, Elli, Armando, and Hans. He had prepared small medicine pouches as protection for each of them.

The spiritual nature of the medicine pouches reminded Hans of the gold cross Anne had given him for Elli. She took it with a shy smile, and a single tear rolled down her cheek. No, Elli wasn't alone anymore; She had made friends who were willing to ride with her and risk their own lives for her and for justice. The lawman's beautiful daughter felt guilty about it, and Armando sensed it. He took the necklace and gently put it around her neck.

"I have no better plans, remember? We are here because we chose it. There is no reason for you to feel guilty. Danger is everywhere, Miss Townsend. All of us knew we might lose our lives when we moved out West for good. But I am sure I can speak for all of us when I say we learned how important loyal friends are. If not for you, I wouldn't be here now. Naiche has fought for his family his entire life, and Hans needs to protect not only you but also his own family and ranch, hence his future. Those scalawags are a constant danger to all of us. Plus, don't forget, we all are friends, and they didn't only kill your father, but they tried to kill you. That is unforgivable."

Elli looked into the serious faces of the men standing around her, tears of gratitude filling her eyes. Each one showed the same determined expression.

My father would have been proud to see these men riding with me, she thought. Then she smiled at them and whispered, "Let's get them, it is payback time."

Elli had pinned her father's sheriff's badge to her new, blue blouse. She hadn't cleaned it up; she left her own blood on the badge as a reminder about whom she was dealing with. This time she wouldn't walk blindly into a trap and would not be stopped until she saw the men who had murdered her beloved father, dead.

CHAPTER TWENTY-SEVEN

* * *

AFTER A FEW HOURS' RIDE THEY ARRIVED AT THE SIGHT WHERE THE ARMY transport had been robbed. They found the abandoned wagon, but the dead soldiers were gone. Their compadres had buried them farther up the hill. Elli and Naiche looked at the fresh graves. Six soldiers lost their lives here. The Apache chief pointed toward some big rocks close by.

"They must have waited for them behind those boulders. I am sure they shot them in the back. Not a warrior's way. Cowards they are."

Elli nodded. "That would explain why they were able to succeed despite being outnumbered by the soldiers. They must have set up the same trap like they did close to Yuma when they got my father and his deputy. They seem to be well-informed. But I still wonder how they knew I was coming to the Nichols Ranch."

Armando walked up to them. "I think I can answer that question. That guy who told you about the Nichols Ranch and the planned cattle rustling to begin informed them you were coming. The owner of the restaurant told me that he had been seen with outlaws in the past, and I'm pretty sure he helped them set up the trap."

"Well, if that's the case, then the Texas Logan Gang has four members and not three as we had always assumed," Elli said. Armando nodded.

They watched Naiche kneel to examine the tracks. Fortunately, it hadn't rained so they were still visible. The Apache walked around for a little while, then came back to them. "The soldiers trampled all over the place, but I found the tracks of four horses leading away in the direction south. Two horses carry a heavier weight."

Armando thought about it, scratching his chin. "That could be the weight of the stolen Winchesters the soldiers told me about. I heard them saying that the transport didn't only contain gold but extra guns as well. They will surely try to sell them to the banditos in the Mexican territory. It will slow them down to sell the loot and celebrate with some women of easy morals."

"Well, let them celebrate as much as they want because it will be their last hog-killing time," Elli said, hands clenched into fists above her pistol holster.

They all got back into their saddles and followed the trail. Thanks to Naiche and his outstanding tracking talents, they never lost their prey. They rode long hours and camped in the wilderness, avoiding towns until they finally reached the border territory where they rode into the small town of Rio Gusto and stayed overnight.

In Rio Gusto people were used to all kinds of strangers so the posse didn't draw much attention. However, they were an uncommonly mixed group with a beautiful white woman in Apache clothes, an Apache riding with white people, a Spaniard, and a typical rancher. But folks in that settlement didn't ask questions. The area was dangerous, and it was safer to stick to one's own business.

The group paid feed and boxes for their horses and Naiche stayed overnight in the livery stable. Not only did he feel more comfortable keeping an eye on the horses, but being in the white people's town made him uneasy. He hadn't forgotten the incident in Jerome, and knew he was in danger as an Apache in Arizona as well as in Mexico. Many of his brothers raided the area regularly. Countless killings had occurred on both sides.

Naiche often wished they could return to the happy, untroubled times of his ancestors before the white man had set foot into this country. Sadly, he knew things would never be the same again for the Apaches, or for any other tribe for that matter.

However, Naiche had convinced his band that being friends with the Snebly family and Elli Townsend might be important for his tribe one day.

The Apache fed the horses and watched Elli's stallion, Thunder who was a splendid animal. The warrior was glad that they had saved the horse as well.

Hans brought some food over from the small cantina for his Apache friend after he had enjoyed the chili and tortillas himself. Mexican food was a welcome change from the daily ranch meals. After paying he scooped a generous portion onto a tin plate for his friend. The whole Snebly family cared deeply for the chief and now even more as he had saved their new friend from Yuma.

***

Elli and Armando stayed at the cantina trying to figure out what to do next. Elli had hidden her father's sheriff's badge before they rode into town. She didn't want to raise sand and she surely didn't want Texas Logan to get wind that she had survived his attack. That was a fact he would get to know soon enough—maybe when she was aiming the barrel of her loaded gun at him. She had two open accounts with this man, and she would settle them at any cost.

Her Spanish friend touched her arm gently, pulling her out of the dark thoughts. She looked up at him.

He pointed toward a fellow with Mexican features at the bar of the cantina drinking tequila. The bartender spoke to him but obviously the man was madder than a wet hen. He tossed a coin on the bar and stomped out of the cantina.

Elli shrugged her shoulders. "Looked like he was really upset over something."

Armando agreed. "Let's go. Time to get some rest before we ride again tomorrow. It's going to be a long, tough day again. How is that wound of yours? Are you okay with the extended hours in the saddle?"

She smiled at him and had to admit it felt nice for someone to constantly worry over her well-being. "Yes, I'm okay. A bit sewn up, but the pain is not too bad. I'll get some sleep now and tomorrow I'll be fresh and ready to ride again."

As they walked toward the small, shabby accommodation, they saw the man from the cantina standing in the street, yelling at a cowboy. "I don't mean to bother you but I have to find my wife. I will not give up until I bring her home again.

You might as well tell that to the dirty bastard who kidnapped my esposa, Juanita. If he hurts her, I'll kill him and, believe me, he'll suffer a lot before he dies."

The other man shook his head. "I told you. I have no idea where Logan and his gang rode to. I didn't know they were after your wife, either. Now go and stall your mug, hombre!"

The buckaroo turned around and walked away from the

Mexican who stood in the middle of the road. He looked devastated and finally walked toward a small house at the end of the street.

"Do you think that was about Texas Logan?" Elli wondered.

"I'm not sure, but let's check on this man in the morning after he has sobered up. Right at the moment it might not be a good idea to approach him as strangers. He sure has a barking iron in his house."

They walked to the boarding house where they'd rented rooms for the night. Hans met them at the door, and they told him what they'd just witnessed. Then they all went to their rooms to rest for a few hours.

The next morning, they met with Naiche at the cantina and had a hearty breakfast. The food wasn't anything special, but it would keep them full until late afternoon.

When they had finished, they walked toward the rental stables and ran into the very same Mexican they had seen airin' his lungs in the street the previous evening.

"Bueno' día', Señor," Armando greeted him in a friendly manner. Elli expected a harsh reply, but to her surprise, the man turned and greeted the group, tipped his hat, and bowed his head at Elli.

"I am sorry if we address you so bluntly, but we overheard your conversation yesterday, and it seemed that you were in some kind of trouble. May we help you somehow?"

Armando played it smart, Elli thought. The man watched them, pondering whether he should talk this unusual looking group of strangers. He must have decided he needed any help he could get.

"Let's go to my house over there." He pointed toward the small house with an inviting porch and a picket fence around it. They followed and he motioned to the rocking chair, offering it to Elli, who sat down with a smile. She loved rocking chairs.

"I am called José Hernandez. My father has a big hacienda in this area, and my mother is from the East Coast of Mexico. I have lived in this town for five years with my beautiful wife, Juanita. A few days back a gang of four outlaws came here.

They were drinking and misbehaving like so many others do in this territory. However, they seemed more dangerous than the usual cattle rustlers you see around here.

This town draws a lot of road agents who dodge the law. One of them laid eyes on my Juanita. The others called him Darrell."

Elli jumped up from the rocking chair, but Armando motioned for her to sit and wait for the whole story. José continued. "The other day Juanita helped out at the cantina. She is an excellent cook. However, that Darrell fellow bragged that he had found his sweet señorita for the night and started to harass my wife. I was out of town that day helping my father at the hacienda. When I returned home, Juanita wasn't there. Someone told me that the scum had left town, but the fellow called Darrell had stayed back a few hours. When Juanita walked home, he must have grabbed her, pulled her onto his saddle, and rode off with her. No one was able to do anything about it. It happened too fast. But I think the buckaroo I argued with yesterday knows those banditos. He must have a clue about where they went, and where I hopefully can find my beloved wife."

***

Armando noticed the man's fearful expression. He understood too well what was going on in his heart.

The fear of losing his wife and that she might have been

raped or even killed must be driving him crazy.

Armando, who had experienced the murder of his own wife, looked at Elli. She nodded and turned toward José. "It's time to lay our cards on the table," she said. "We're looking for the same curly wolves." José Hernandez stared at her in disbelief.

Elli told him the main facts of her story, her father's murder, her assault, near death, and about the people who had helped and saved her, including Naiche was following the conversation silently from the other side of the porch. Elli also told José that the Texas Logan Gang had robbed the bank in Jerome and the military wagon a few weeks back.

The Mexican jumped up. "Something has to be done about them! Let's go and get them, I'll ride with you. That way our chances are even better. I'll kill the bastards with my bare hands."

Armando smiled at him and said "Careful, the law is watching you." Then he laughed at José's puzzled look and pointed toward Elli. "Although she calls herself Elli, I would like to introduce you to the late Sheriff Townsend's daughter and Deputy of Yuma, Eleonora Townsend."

Elli looked at Armando not understanding what he was talking about.

Finally, he produced a telegram from his pocket.

"In the whole confusion when I tried to find you, I totally forgot this telegram. It is from my friend and former U.S. Marshal Larson whom you met in Tucson. He has ordered the town of Yuma to appoint you as an official Deputy of a U.S. Marshal. You are covered by the law now. This is an official posse and the law is with you, Eleonora Townsend. You are taking action on behalf of your father and the Arizona Territory and in the name of the law he stood for."

She didn't know what to say. Armando had legalized her vendetta and she hadn't anything to fear from the law. They exchanged glances and formed a mutual understanding that only death could stop their mission. One would have the other one's back—for good and forever.

***

José shook his head in disbelief. "A female deputy?"

Hans looked at the Mexican. "Yes, sir, and a hell of a fighter, too."

José Hernandez looked at her and saw the ice-cold stare of Elli's blue eyes. *Yes, this woman means business indeed.*

He slowly got up, walked into the house to pick up his Peacemaker and Winchester, and returned to the group on his porch. "Let's ride and get them bastards!"

No one questioned his joining the group. They silently accepted him into the posse.

CHAPTER TWENTY-EIGHT

***

BEFORE THEY LEFT TOWN, HANS AND ARMANDO VISITED THE LOCAL BROTHEL TO try and find out some information about where Logan's mob might have gone after leaving Rio Gusto. Their hunch was right that some of the gang members had stopped here for entertainment. Armando could barely keep his rage under control when he heard that one John Harker had been a customer of the Mexican sporting girls as well. John Harker, the very same feller who had lured Elli into a deadly trap.

One of the girls told Armando in Spanish that, although Harker was handsome, he was a brutal customer to have and she was glad when he left the house of ill fame. One lady of the line told them the gang was off to the town of Naco to trade "some goods," whatever that meant.

Armando was sure that those "goods" must be the stolen weapons from the robbery of the army transport. At least now they knew which direction to take. Armando paid the women well. They were surprised to receive his coins although he and Hans hadn't enjoyed their services. The two men went back to the others, hopped on their horses, and they headed toward Naco.

Later the posse camped close to a creek. Naiche and Armando fished for their dinner. Elli and Hans watered and tended to the horses while José stood guard to make sure nobody would try to rob them. It was a dangerous area and often looted by road agents or renegade Indians.

Soon the mouthwatering smell of grilled fish filled the air. A muted conversation among the friends added to the peaceful atmosphere of the evening. But none of them forgot that they were on a dangerous mission. All of them could be killed, and all were aware of it. Elli touched her chest where she had been shot. It hurt and she felt lightheaded. She knew she had to get some rest. Armando looked at her and pointed to his saddle and blanket. "Lie down and sleep, Elli. Hans and I will take over the first watch."

She agreed, went to his saddle, and wrapped herself in the blanket, enjoying the scent of him. She dozed off immediately. Her long hair fell in dark waves over his saddle.

"She's a brave woman," José remarked. Armando nodded.

"I'm scared that I'll find my wife dead or raped," the Mexican whispered. "How could I ever handle that?"

Armando looked at him. "It is an almost unbearable pain. But you have to keep your head clear. Chances are we will find her alive in time. Don't give up too early. If she is still alive that should be all that matters to you, even if they laid hands on her." José looked away as tears filled his eyes.

Armando got up, patted his shoulder, and motioned to a spot near the campfire. "Rest now; we will wake you later to take over the second shift guarding the camp."

While Armando and Hans were watching over the safety of their compadres, Elli, Naiche, and José tried to get some precious sleep before the next day would challenge them again.

CHAPTER TWENTY-NINE

***

WHEN THE GROUP GOT UP WITH FIRST DAYLIGHT, THEY LEFT CAMP WITHOUT eating. They were eager to get to Naco. But after one hour's ride, the Apache chief held up a hand and stopped the group. He rode off to the right through some brush. After a few minutes he returned, a torn piece of red cloth in his hand.

"There is the track of one horse leading away from the others toward that hill there." He pointed westwards. "That horse carries the weight of two people and I found this."

"Oh, my God!" Hernandez gasped. "Juanita wore a red skirt the day she was kidnapped."

The desperate husband was about to give his horse the spurs, but Armando held him back. "Slowly, Hoss, if we act too impulsively, we might give the guy a warning or, even worse, enough time to kill your wife. The good news is she was most likely still alive when he passed through the brush there because it wouldn't make sense at all to carry a dead body on his horse."

That said, José calmed down a bit. "God, I pray we find her in time." He was devastated when he imagined what his wife might have been through already.

Elli looked at Armando and the others. "Well, my father is buried but that woman might still be alive. I think we should go after this one first, and continue the chase for Texas Logan later." They all agreed, and Hernandez looked at them gratefully for the unexpected help and loyalty from these people.

So, they changed direction and rode toward the hill while Naiche rode ahead to read the clues on the ground. He stopped his horse and motioned them to dismount as quietly as possible. They walked over to him. Their Apache friend pointed toward a rough hut on the other side of the hill. A single horse grazed next to it, but there was no sign of people. The members of the posse slowly sneaked closer to the cabin while Hans stayed back near the horses to make sure they didn't take off if spooked by gunfire.

They took cover behind boulders and mesquite bushes, slowly creeping forward. They had almost reached cabin when a woman's piercing scream filled the air.

"Juanita!" José yelled and jumped up.

"Damn, you fool!" Armando called after him, but it was too late. He, Elli, and Naiche left their cover to run after Hernandez, trying their best to protect him.

The door to the hut flung open and Darrell Lenny stood in the door frame peering around. When he saw four people running toward him, he quickly turned and closed the door behind him.

"If you come any closer, she will take a bullet!" he yelled behind the door.

"You saphead," Armando hissed at José.

"She's my wife! You would've done the same if you heard your wife scream like that," Hernandez defended himself. The Spaniard had to admit that the fellow was right about that.

Elli remained calm and motioned for Naiche to make his way to the backside of the crude cabin while she got hold of the outlaw's horse.

"The scamp is outnumbered and knows it so he'll probably use her as a hostage to make his way out of here," she whispered. "Get his attention. Naiche will be out back of that lousy looking cabin. The moment Lenny sees me he'll be shocked because they all think I'm dead. Armando! That will be the only moment you have to save Juanita because as soon as he's aware who is after him, he knows he's done for. When that murderer realizes he has nothing to lose, he'll shoot her and try to send us to the bone orchard as well."

Armando knew she was right. The surprise about her survival was their only chance as Darrell Lenny hadn't recognized her yet. Armando looked at José Hernandez who struggled to get his shaking nerves under control. At least, so far, Juanita was still alive. Naiche slowly moved toward the back of the cabin.

From inside, through the cracked door, Darrell shouted angrily, "You'd better pull in your horns! If you let me leave unmolested you can have her back."

Armando watched Elli who had almost reached the bandito's nervous mare. He watched her calming the frightened animal before leading it away from the door. Then Armando shouted back, "Come on out and make sure you do not hurt the woman. We will let you ride away, but we want her unharmed. If anything happens to the lady, you are dead, you hear me?"

"Get away from the door and throw away your guns." The door opened with a shrieking sound, and Juanita appeared, the barrel of a six-gun pressed against her temple.

Juanita's husband almost cried out her name, but Armando whispered, "Hold your horses, for land's sake, we will help her. You have to trust us and remain quiet."

José nodded and managed to hold his emotions in check.

Juanita's eyes were huge as she recognized her husband, but fear held her rapidly beating heart in an deadly grip. Armando and José both held their guns above their heads.

"Toss them away!" Darrell yelled. They obeyed and threw their weapons on the dusty ground—but not far.

Darrell looked around. "Where's my horse?" he yelled. He grew nervous trying to keep an eye on the two guys in front while holding onto the woman who was his ticket to freedom.

"This is going wrong. Something smells fishy," he mumbled. Their boss man Texas Logan always found a way out. He cursed himself for having separated from the group for the sake of having a bit fun with the kidnapped woman. He had always been driven by his taste for Mexican females, and now it had gotten him into serious trouble.

It surprised him to hear his horse snorting. Someone was leading it around the corner, hat pulled down to hide the face.

He wanted to wrestle the woman toward his mare when the stranger leading her slowly pushed back the hat. Darrell couldn't believe what he saw.

There she was, the woman they had ambushed and left behind to die at the Nichols Ranch when Indians attacked. How could it be? The lawman's daughter had been mortally wounded. He had seen it with his own eyes.

"What the hell! You're supposed to be dead … Logan shot you!" He stared at her, confusion and fear showing in his eyes.

At that moment, José Hernandez and his new Spanish

friend moved toward the outlaw. Darrell yanked Juanita around by the arm, and she cried out in pain.

"Let her go!" The fierce order came from Elli, and Darrell pointed his six-shooter at her, away from Juanita. Suddenly Darrell Lenny screamed in pain as the silent knife of Naiche sunk into his shoulder. The outlaw dropped his gun.

Armando knocked Darrell down with a sharp blow from his right fist. José caught his stumbling wife Juanita before she hit the ground.

The woman looked miserable. Her blouse had been torn, and her face was bruised. One eye was swollen shut, and dried blood covered her upper lip. She wept and placed her hands on her husband's chest, pushing him away. He wanted to catch her eye, to hug her, but she didn't meet his gaze. José Hernandez understood right away that she felt ashamed. There was only one reason why his wife would feel humiliated, and raging fury seized him.

Armando tried to hold him back from attacking Darrell Lenny. "Let the law handle it."

Elli approached Darrell Lenny. "Well, Darrell, there's a German saying 'You always meet twice.' Isn't that the truth?"

"I didn't try to kill you. It was all Logan's idea. He was also the one who shot your father."

Elli was deeply disgusted by this coward. "Well, too bad. You'll face justice anyway. You robbed the bank in Jerome and killed the soldiers of that transport for the fort, kidnapped this lady, and, from what I see, also raped her. You have no right at all to expect mercy. I have enough witnesses, and although I'm not a judge, I have the authority to arrest you."

"Please, I need a doctor! That rotten Apache tried to kill

me with his knife. I'm bleeding to death."

"Well, I'd say you got what you deserved," Elli answered coolly.

Armando gripped Darrell's wrists and tied them behind his back. Then he pulled Naiche's knife from the outlaw's shoulder and wasn't bothered in the least when Darrell cried out in pain.

He cleaned the knife in the grass. As he handed it to his Apache friend, Armando observed the back of the outlaw's shirt. He was indeed bleeding heavily, but Armando didn't feel sorry for him.

"We'll hand him over to the law in Naco where he can await his trial," Elli announced.

They watched Hans walk down the hill with their horses. Juanita barely looked at them, so big was her shame. But her husband held her tight in his arms. "Juanita, I am so thankful God sent me these friends, and that we were able to save you. Nothing else matters. Nobody will ever take away the love I feel for you. Whatever happened while you were kidnapped is in the past. And, none of it was your fault. There is no need to feel ashamed."

Darrell Lenny started to giggle and was about to say something when Elli pulled her pistol from her holster and smacked him across his face. "One word, you dirty beast, and I'll shoot you right here, and say you tried to flee from the law." Her voice was deadly calm and the man knew she meant it. For a moment he remained silent while his slpiy lip bled onto his shirt. Then he turned to her.

"Damn woman, Logan should have killed you right away," he cursed.

"Yes, he should have because now it's going to be the other way around," she hissed back at him.

CHAPTER THIRTY

***

THEY GOT ONTO THEIR HORSES. JUANITA RODE WITH JOSÉ. HE HELD HER SECURE-ly in his saddle. Darrell rode on his own horse between Naiche and Hans who had their guns ready in case he tried to escape.

As it got dark, they camped close to the town of Naco where they were supposed to find Logan and Pete Lenny as well as John Harker. They used a rope to tie Darrell against a tree. They all were hungry and Naiche was able to hunt two rabbits. The night was cool and they were all exhausted by the day's events.

When they raised from their blankets the next morning, ready to ride to Naco, Hans called them over to their prisoner. He pointed to the apparently still sleeping man.

"He's dead—must have bled to death." Nobody showed any emotion.

Finally, Hernandez turned around. "He got what he deserved, nobody escapes God's justice," he said as he put and arm around Juanita and walked toward his horse.

Armando and Naiche both watched Elli. "That's number one," she whispered. They buried the ruthless gang member under the tree where he had died the previous night. Hans built a crude wooden cross and left it blank.

They saddled up and rode toward their destination of Naco. Juanita now rode Darrell's horse. She seemed calmer since Darrell's demise, and said she felt safe among these people who had helped her husband to free her.

It might be tricky if Texas Logan saw Juanita, he would immediately recognize Darrell's horse as well as the kidnapped woman and wonder where Darrell was. He would become alarmed right away and realize something was the matter.

Elli suggested that Armando and Hans, who were unknown to the men who rode with Logan, ride into Naco first, and try to find out if Logan and his pack were still in town. Meanwhile, Juanita, José, and Elli would have to hide in one of the buildings close to the city limits.

Hans and Armando decided to go to the town's saloon and ask around about the murderers. While they had a shot of bottled courage at the bar they poked around.

The town's saloon hosted a considerable number of drifters, saddle tramps, gamblers, and soiled doves sitting at the tables. The place was loud and busy and thick with cigar smoke. It was easy to see that this settlement was a gathering place for fellers dodging the law.

"We have to be careful how we ask questions here," Armando whispered to Hans.

His friend agreed. "Damn straight. Dangerous crowd here."

Hans walked over to some mean-looking cowboys and sat down at their table. "Howdy fellows, may I join your poker game?"

Armando watched and wondered what Snebly was up to. One of the guys shrugged his shoulder. "If you have money, why not? We don't play for high stakes though. If you want to lose a lot more money you have to go over to the faro table. The guy who holds the bank is a real 'speeler.' "

The other men laughed at that and Hans joined them. "No interest. I need my money. I came here because I heard I could buy some new Winchesters at reasonable prices. So, I'd better keep an eye on my dinero."

The three buckaroos looked at each other.

"Well, we happen to know someone who sells brand new Winchesters, best quality, so to speak. If we introduce you to the trader, how much would you be willing to pay us?"

Hans scratched his chin. "Well, I'd have to ask my partner over there. But I'm sure we could pay you a fair amount since you'd save us time looking for contacts."

"We'll speak to our friend and see what we can do. Are you staying in town?" Hans nodded.

"Then let's meet here tomorrow morning."

Hans thanked them and bought them a round of tongue oil. They showed their appreciation with toasts. But he skipped the poker game.

Snebly walked back to the bar and informed his companion. "That was a smart move, my friend," the Spaniard admitted. "Let's go back to the boarding house and tell the others."

On the way to their accommodation, they passed the local bordello. Armando asked Hans to wait and carefully pointed to the entrance. "That guy over there leaving the bed-house looks just like Elli had described that John Harker flannel mouth."

"You mean the one who sent her into the trap at the Nichols Ranch?" the surprised farmer asked.

"I'm pretty sure. Elli would recognize him right away,

but I get the feeling that we are on the right track."

"Well, we have to make sure he doesn't accidently run into her. It would blow our whole plan about surprising them. But maybe we can get her to identify the guy somehow, just to be sure," Hans suggested.

The two friends hastily returned to their rooms for the night to inform the others. They filled in their friends about what they discovered about the outlaws and the planned meeting with the buckaroos the next day.

Armando gently took Elli's arm and walked her to the window of their boarding house. He pointed down the road toward the brothel. "Can you see the street in front of the bordello on the left?"

"Yes, but what for?" She had no idea what he wanted to show her. But then Elli saw a man lighting a match at the wooden wall. He lit his cigarette and turned toward the petroleum lamp that hung next to the entrance to attract male visitors.

Elli gasped as she saw the face of the stranger who had taken off his hat and pushed back his hair. She recognized John Harker right away. Elli Townsend wanted to go after him, but Armando held her back. "If he sees you and escapes, he can warn Logan and the other Lenny brother. We have to make sure he can't escape, you understand me?"

She shook her head. "He's within our grasp now."

"Listen, if we arrest him now, he might have a way to send word to Logan even if he is behind bars. There are only two ways out. Either you let him run now or we have to make sure he can't talk to anyone anymore."

Her eyes grew huge. "You mean we should murder him?"

"They tried to murder you, and he was part of the plot, remember?"

She stared out the window, battling with herself. On one side there was the wish for revenge for her father and for what they had done to her, but, on the other hand, she'd always obeyed the law that her father represented. To arrest them and see them hang was one thing, but cold-blooded murder …

"Elli, you almost died because he lured you into a trap."

"Yes, I know but I'm not a murderer, Armando. I'm a deputy, and what counts even more, I have to respect what my father taught me about following the law."

They observed Harker walking across the street and disappearing into a house quite close to their lodging. "We should follow him and see who lives there," Naiche said. "Maybe it is even that Texas Logan's accommodation." So both men, Naiche and Armando left the boarding house and moved cautiously, remaining on the darker side of the road.

As they came to the small Victorian home, they saw light in the living room. A young woman seemed entangled in a heated argument with John Harker. She was crying and their conversation soon erupted into a loud fight.

"Why did you go into the brothel to those women without any morals? You said you felt for me, and we were planning to get married soon, have you forgotten that?"

Her pretty face was flushed with anger. He just laughed at her and turned to get a glass of whiskey from the counter. The Apache shook his head. "A man of wrong women and firewater. I think that lady is in danger, my white brother." Armando knew Naiche was right.

The scene was out of control as the woman stormed toward Harker and hit him on his back with her tiny fists. He threw the glass against the wall and flung her across the room.

"I'll teach you a lesson to attack me, woman," he yelled

at her. His face was a mask of brutality. He removed his belt and started to beat her severely as she screamed for help. That was enough for Armando. He went to the front door and kicked it in. Naiche was right behind him. Harker was taken by surprise, but only for a few seconds. He pulled out his Bowie knife and went straight for the tall Spaniard.

Naiche quickly ran over to the confused woman on the floor and helped her to her feet. Her face was bleeding, and red streaks showed on her cheeks. The lady trembled with fear. Harker overpowered Armando in his fury. They both fell on the floor and rolled over and over.

At that very moment Armando's mind held the image of a fatally wounded Elli fighting for her life. Anger and rage took a hold of him and he started to beat John Harker mercilessly. "I will kill you with my bare hands, you bastard."

The outlaw tried to crawl away from his frenzied opponent. He had regained his footing when Armando grabbed his jacket and wrenched the criminal toward him.

Harker lost his balance and crashed to the floor face first. A muffled cry escaped him and he remained there in silence, not moving at all.

Elli's friend was panting hard, recovering from the fight. The blind rage he felt for the person who had tricked Elli into a near-fatal ambush began to dissipate.

Naiche turned over Harker's body. Blood soaked the crook's shirt. He had fallen onto his own knife. The very knife he used against Armando had turned into a deadly weapon against himself.

"Justice never fails," whispered the Apache leader. "Let's leave this house quick before anybody sees us. We'd better take the woman along. Elli can explain everything to her," Naiche suggested.

Armando, still breathing hard, agreed and picked up

his hat while the Apache chief led the shocked woman out of the house. Nobody saw them. Armando stood in the doorframe and turned around. He stared at the dead body lying in his own blood. "Number two," he whispered. Then he pulled the door shut.

Elli was surprised when they entered the hotel room with another woman. It was obvious that she had been beaten and was in shock. Naiche quickly told her what had happened while Juanita tended to the unknown lady's bleeding lip.

"I had no choice, Elli," said Armando. "He tried to stab me with his Bowie."

"Did you kill him, Armando?" she asked.

"No, he fell onto his own knife when he lost his balance. But I admit I am not sad about it. He got what he deserved. You can ask Naiche. He saw the fight."

She brushed his cheek. "I have no reason to doubt your word, my dear friend." He was surprised by her touch, but it felt good and warm against his skin.

Elli turned around to the weeping female. She took her hand and asked the others, except Juanita, to leave the room. Once they were alone the crying lady introduced herself as Isabell Carson. Deputy Elli Townsend patiently told her the entire story, and how John Harker had been involved since Jerome. Juanita joined in by telling her that Texas Logan's gang member had taken her hostage and raped her and it had been Elli and her friends who had saved her from being killed or sold as a slave to a local brothel.

Isabell was shocked, but she wasn't really surprised. "I sensed something was wrong for quite a while. His absences and mysterious business trips always left me behind in doubt. Sometimes he would be gone for weeks. I thought it had to do with other women, but now I see he was a criminal and a scamp. I'm glad he's gone. John wasn't a good man. He was rather brutal and mean, and I'm sure it would have gotten worse if I had married him."

Elli agreed. There was no point in sugarcoating facts. She invited Isabell to sleep in her room for the night. "Isabell, it's important they find his body as late as possible. Is someone else living in that house?"

She shook her head. "I'm alone. My parents are both dead. It's my house. Nobody goes there and as long as I show up in town, nobody would assume anything is wrong."

Elli hugged her. "Now try to get some rest. Hans Snebly and my friend Armando will meet some shady cowboys tomorrow who, hopefully, lead us to Logan and the other Lenny brother. However, we remaining people in our group have to hide the entire day to make sure we surprise them. We don't want them to recognize us too early. Soon it'll be judgement day for them."

Isabell understood how important this was. She tried to get some rest and felt safe in the female deputy's room.

The events of the evening and the fact that her fiancé was dead left her in turmoil nevertheless. Isabell told Elli that she wasn't sure what bothered her more: losing him forever or the fact that he had been a dangerous outlaw and cheater.

Elli watched the young woman toss and turn in her sleep and felt sorry for her. Finally, she drifted off into a shallow slumber herself. Armando and Hans caught up on sleep with their loaded guns next to them while Naiche checked on the horses in the rental stable one more time. José Hernandez kept an eye on the two rooms making sure the women were safe. Naiche bunked in the stable. It would have caused unwanted trouble if he had slept in the boarding house.

CHAPTER THIRTY-ONE

* * *

THE NEXT DAY HANS WENT INTO ISABELL'S HOUSE. HE PLANNED TO HIDE THE body of John Harker and to get some clothes for her. The poor woman had gone through a lot. Hans imagined the fragile looking, petite blonde and wondered how a man could raise a hand against any woman. He had been brought up to respect females. When Hans entered the house, he saw the dead outlaw lying in a puddle of dried blood and grabbed him by his boots to drag him to the room in the back. Then he went through the lady's closet and got her an extra dress and a pair of riding coulottes as well.

"I hope she can ride in case she has to come along with us," he muttered.

On an impulse he took an elegant engraved silver hairbrush which lay in front of a dressing mirror. It felt strange for him to be holding female belongings in his rough farmer's hands. The items smelled of violets and he smiled. The fragrance reminded him of his late mother's flowerbed back home.

Armando and José organized some breakfast and explained to the boarding house owner that the ladies riding with them didn't feel well. They wanted to make sure that the townspeople didn't ask any nosy questions. The man running the place winked at them. "Women and their sicknesses. I'll send my wife up and she can fix some bacon, eggs, and biscuits. It'll cost you extra though."

Armando paid in advance, and a little while later Elli, Isabell, and Juanita enjoyed a hearty breakfast in their room while José and the Spaniard ate downstairs. They kept some food for Hans who hadn't returned from Isabell's house.

When Snebly finally got back, he went straight to the women's room. Isabell was still pale, but she had her emotions under control. When Hans gave her the clothes and her hairbrush, he blushed and she smiled at him.

"That was very kind of you. Is he ...?" She let the question trail off.

He looked at her. "I hid him well and yes, he's dead. You have nothing to fear. John Harker will never hurt you again."

"Thank you, Mister Snebly."

"Call me Hans, please."

"Well, then, Hans. I am Isabell." He nodded. Armando and Elli watched them from across the room. Hans blushed again.

Armando took Hans aside. "Let's walk around town a bit, Hans. Maybe we'll get lucky and will hear some news about Texas Logan before we meet those guys from yesterday's poker table."

Meanwhile Isabell decided to visit a friend of hers and to show herself around town a bit to keep people from thinking that something might be wrong. She went to the local mercantile and bought a new blouse for Juanita whose clothes had been torn to pieces by her attacker.

Naiche gave Elli a pouch containing some herbs. "Try to

get the owner's wife to make you tea from this. It will give you strength for what you have to face soon. Remember, you still recover from a close encounter with death."

Elli looked at the Apache, nodded and thanked him. She was touched by the loyalty of her friends and knew she needed these people. Her gut feeling told her that the moment to face Texas Logan drew near.

Armando and Hans walked by the blacksmith, the local mercantile, and finally the bordello where they had seen John Harker the previous night. One of the girls talked to them, trying to lure them into the house of ill repute. They paid her a coin and hoped she would reveal what she knew about John Harker or Texas Logan and Pete Lenny.

But she became nervous when she heard those names and didn't want to answer any questions. It was obvious that she was scared to death of the outlaws.

Hans explained that they were definitely no friends of either one so she shyly pointed at another girl standing close by. An ugly red scar disfigured her pretty face. It went all the way down from her right eye to her jawbone.

"Texas Logan did that. He's extremely brutal and dangerous. None of us dares to speak up against him or deny him anything at all. He is unpredictable. As for John Harker, yes, he rides with them from time to time. Why wouldn't he? After all, Texas Logan is his nephew."

Armando stared at her. "Is that so? His nephew?"

She nodded. "I've got to go now. I'm not allowed to just talk to a man."

The two men thanked her. "Looks like that scum really got what he deserved, right?"

The Spanish rancher agreed. "I wish I had killed him myself though."

Hans slapped his friend on his shoulder. "I know brother, I know. God punished him, and you won't have to live with the guilt of killing him."

"Well, let's go over to the saloon and see if those saddle tramps are there," Armando suggested. They both went straight to the bar and ordered a beer.

They wanted to remain sober and refused the offered corn juice when the two other fellows arrived.

"We spoke to our friend. It happens that he can offer you twenty brand-new Winchesters, Army quality," the elder one bragged. "Hope you have enough kelter with you."

Armando smiled at him. "We are not that blue-eyed to trust you right away like that. Let's meet in the afternoon with your friend. I want to see and test the weapons first. After all, some guns don't always function the way they should."

"Do you call me a liar, sir?" The elder guy was offended by Armando's doubts.

"Not at all, but we want to make sure we get what we pay for. You would do the same if you were in our boots," Hans interjected. The other buckaroo tucked at his angry compadre's sleeve.

"He's right. We'd do the same, and anyway Logan told us to bring him out to the cave."

"Well then, we'll have a drink or two until you return with your horses, and we'll show you the way."

They shook hands on it. Then Hans and Armando left the saloon.

"What do you think of it?" Hans asked his friend.

"I don't trust them. I'm sure they will bring us to Logan and then try to send us right to the boot yard so that these scalawags can keep the weapons and the money." Hans Snebly knew his companion was right.

"Well, they probably think they outnumber us as it

would be the two of us against their four. What they don't know is, that we are four as well counting Naiche and Elli in. They would have to follow us a safe distance so they could jump in when the gun fight starts."

When the two friends arrived back at the boarding house, they spoke to the others, especially to Hernandez. "José, we don't want to pull you into this so you might as well stay back and make sure that Juanita and Isabell are safe. Your wife is not allowed to show up in town until we are done with Texas Logan and Pete Lenny; they would both recognize her right away and get suspicious."

Armando didn't like it at all that Elli would ride with them, but it was her vendetta after all. He knew too well that no one or nothing, would prevent her from taking revenge.

The horses were saddled and waiting at the stable. The men and Elli had their weapons loaded, and their grim expressions showed that they were ready to face their enemies. Isabell Carson returned to the rented room just as they were about to leave. She looked worried for the folks who had been so kind to her.

Hans smiled. "We'll be back safely, don't worry about us."

She looked at him and said, "You'd better keep that promise, sir!"

On sudden impulse Hans hugged the fragile looking woman, then quickly turned away before she saw his blushing cheeks.

CHAPTER THIRTY-TWO

✳ ✳ ✳

ELLI GOT INTO THE SADDLE, HER FATHER'S HOLSTER AROUND HER SLIM HIPS, his sheriff's badge pinned to her blouse and an additional rifle in her hand. Chief Naiche rode beside her. There was a strong bond between them and neither would hesitate to die for the other. They had been hiding behind the barn until they saw Armando, Hans, and the two cowboys ride out of town, then they quickly followed.

Logan's men led Armando and Hans into a rugged side canyon where they saw smoke curling up behind boulders farther up the cliff on the right.

"You'll have to get off your horses here and leave them behind," one of the cowboys ordered.

Armando pointed at both of them to walk ahead. "Since you know the way you may as well lead." They climbed to a small cave under an overhanging flat rock. Pete and Texas Logan jumped to their feet, guns ready to shoot the intruders.

The other two fellers held up their hands assuring them they were the expected company. "We're bringing the gents who want to buy your rifles, Logan."

The gang leader looked at Hans, then with some hesitation at Armando. *Obviously, the Spanish fellow is more dangerous,* he thought. Texas Logan asked them what they needed the rifles for. Armando told them a story out of the blue without even hesitating. He was an intelligent man and had expected the question.

"I run a big ranch and need to get rid of some renegade Indians once and for all."

"Why?" Texas Logan asked.

"The bastards stole my wife. Oh hell, I know I can buy a Mexican sage hen any time, but they ran off with two of my best stallions and three of my broodmares as well, and that is unforgivable!"

Texas Logan and Pete Lenny laughed, a cold laughter that never touched their eyes. Hans hadn't the slightest doubt that they were cold-blooded murderers who wouldn't hesitate to assassinate a sheriff and his beautiful daughter.

"You're right about that; a good horse is always worth more than a wife," Logan said while his cruel laughter shook his shoulders again. Armando clenched his fists, striving to keep his emotions under control. He was tempted to beat that devil to death with his bare hands.

"Come on over and have a look at the rifles then." Pete bent down and opened two heavy wooden boxes. In each lay ten gleaming, brand new Winchesters, well-oiled, along with a couple of cartridge boxes.

Hans whistled through his teeth. "Where did you get these?" he asked while taking one out of the box to check its quality.

"Let's say it was a gift from the Army," Pete laughed.

"Shut your big bazoo, Pete!" Texas Logan yelled at him. Pete shied away immediately like an cringing dog.

Armando searched for a way to delay the trade. He

needed to make sure Elli and Naiche were close enough
to join the fight when the scene got out of hands. He had
no doubt that Texas Logan would kill them as soon as he
held the money for the Winchesters in his hands.

"If one of your helpers would go down to my saddlebags
and fetch the best bottle of whiskey in these parts, we could
seal the deal," Armando offered with a sly smile.

Logan looked at the elder of the two cattle rustlers
and nodded. Immediately the fellow turned and climbed
down to the horses that waited below the cave. After all,
a bottle of fine whiskey was too tempting to pass up for
rough outlaws.

When he arrived at the horses and started searching the
saddlebags, Naiche, who had hidden behind a boulder, sent
him into the land of dreams with a hard blow from a rock
against his temple. Elli quickly bound him with a rope and
gagged him with her bandana. Then she climbed toward
the cave using bigger rocks for cover.

She and Naiche both knew they had only a few minutes until Texas Logan and the others realized that the
guy was taking way too long to return with the bottled
"coffin varnish."

"Meanwhile let's talk about the price, sir," the Spanish
noble man started the conversation again.

The mob leader looked at them and scratched his chin.
"Well, how about fifteen dollars each?"

"Way to expensive!" Armando said. He prayed his back
up had already dealt with the outlaw down by the horses.
"I'll give you ten dollars per rifle including the bullets."

Texas Logan thought about it. He knew it was a good
price so he finally agreed, and they shook hands.

Armando felt disgusted at having to touch the hand of
the unscrupulous murderer, but he had to play along for

the time being.

Pete and Logan stood next to their two trading partners while the third outlaw had sneaked away over the rocks. From where they stood neither Hans nor Armando could see that he slowly pulled his pistol from his holster.

"Heck, where is that fool with the corn juice? Probably already drinking some of it alone down there," Pete wondered.

Armando stretched out his hand full of dollars. The very moment that Texas Logan took the money the other outlaw behind them in the rocks pulled the trigger.

Two shots went off at the same time, and the shooting bandit fell to the ground with a bullet hole in his forehead. Blood ran in a tiny trickle across his nose, his eyes staring at the sky. The brigand's bullet had missed Hans by less than an inch.

Then everything happened faster than lightening. "I'm going to get you, dang Iberian dog" Pete yelled aiming at Armando. Texas Logan ran back into the shelter of the cave. Hans and Naiche fired at the same time, mortally wounding Pete with two shots to the chest. He stumbled backwards, dropped his six shooter before he could pull the trigger, and fell like a downed tree.

Armando silently pointed to the cave and Elli, who had appeared from behind a rock and followed him into it.

Her hand gripped her father's Peacemaker. She looked pale but ready to face her father's killer.

Hans surveyed the edge of the cliff above, wondering where the shot that had saved his life had come from. Up there he saw José Hernandez standing with his rifle, waving down at him. The Sedona rancher tipped his hat in deep respect while he watched the Mexican climbing down.

"You saved my life! What are you doing here?" Hans

wanted to know.

"I couldn't stay back; I owe you fellows the life of my beloved wife, and somehow I had to make sure that you return to that lovely blond lady just like you promised her. The women are safe in the boarding house."

They turned toward Pete Lenny, but there wasn't anything they could do for him. The gunshot wounds had soaked his shirt in blood. He must have died as he fell.

"Number three faced justice," Hans remarked as he closed the outlaw's eyes. They took positions at the entrance of the cave in case Texas Logan escape justice from Elli's loaded gun.

Armando motioned Elli to remain silent. He shouted into the cave. "Logan, you tried to get me killed over that deal. You really thought I would be so dumb not to have backup ?"

Armando tried to capture Logan's attention to allow Elli to sneak behind him along the cave's wall between the rocks and niches. He heard a shuffling sound close to him. Texas Logan attacked leaped from the shadows and punched Armando in the face. Without warning, the outlaw had appeared from a dark opening at Armando's left side. The two men fell to the ground and rolled over, trying to knock each other out. Swiftly, Texas Logan gained the advantage on top and pulled his knife.

"I'm going to bed you down anyway, you Spanish bastard!" He panted hard as he tried to bring the down blade to cut Armando's throat. The knife came closer and closer. Elli's friend was in danger of losing his life. From the darkness, a calm, icy voice called out to Logan.

"Drop that knife, now, or I'll shoot your dirty head off!" Taken by surprise at the female voice, Logan spun, pulling back from Armando's chest. The voice sounded familiar.

Slowly Elli walked into the circle of weak daylight fil-
tering into the cave from the entrance. When Logan recognized her, his eyes widened in disbelief. "You? But you're
dead, that's not possible! I shot you! And the Apaches were
there to kill you anyway. How in the world did you get
here? Why are you alive?" He turned pale, understanding
that he was unlikely to escape this cave alive.

She laughed in his face. "Surprise for you, isn't it?
Texas Logan, as a deputy of the Yuma Sheriff's Office, I
hereby arrest you for murdering my father, Sheriff Oscar
Townsend, his deputy, and the coachman in Yuma. You
will stand trial for your crimes including for the robbery of
the bank in Jerome and for murdering the bank official as
well as for the robbery of the army escort and the killing
of the soldiers during that incident. And we can't forget,
you attempted to kill Eleonora Townsend, another U.S.
Deputy. That's me, if you didn't know."

He laughed at her, then stared in bewilderment. It could
not be. He, the great outlaw Texas Logan, being defeated
by a woman. "Your father was a coward, he cried like a
baby when I sent him to boot hill, begged me to keep him
alive like an old woman!" He spit out every word.

Elli felt the rage rushing through her blood and she
slowly cocked the hammer. She would finish him off right
here, right now. He laughed his dirty laughter, still staring
at the barrel of her loaded gun. "You ain't got the sand,
young Missy."

"Elli, hold it!" The gentle voice of Armando seemed to
come from nowhere, but it reached her.

"Not like this, it's too easy and too fast a death for
him. That's what he wants It's the reason he provokes
you. Remember what you told me? Your father was shot
out of the saddle, dragged by his horse. Sheriff Townsend

couldn't have begged for his life. He died bravely on duty, Elli! You want to see this coward hang and beg for his life. The law, Elli, your father's law, remember?"

The pale woman looked down at Texas Logan. "We will throw a nice necktie party for you, you bastard, you'll hang in the town where you killed my father."

He stared at her and knew she meant it. "I should have killed you right away at the Nichols Ranch," he hissed.

"Yes, you should have. Too bad I'm still above snakes, and you will stew in your own juice now. The cards got shuffled differently, and it'll be me who will see you going straight to hell. By the way, the two Lenny brothers and your uncle John Harker are dead as door nails already. We sent them straight to Sam Hill where they belong."

He stared at her in stunned disbelief. She swiftly turned her father's pistol in her hand and whacked it hard against his temple. He sank to the ground like a sack of potatoes.

Deputy Elli Townsend just stood there, trembling with rage and exhaustion. Armando carefully took her into his arms. "You got him; we will make sure he gets what he deserves."

She felt drained and leaned against his broad shoulders gratefully. They dragged Texas Logan out of the cave.

Outside Naiche, Hans, and José waited for them, and helped carry the limb body of the outlaw to their horses. They didn't bother to bury the other two. The mountain lions and coyotes would take care of their bodies.

The third cow hand who had been tied up near the horses was awake by now and begging for mercy. They dragged him along to hand him over to the sheriff of Naco.

When they arrived back in town, they picked up Juanita and Isabell. Both women were relieved to see all of them return alive. It was time to leave the Mexican border town.

José Hernandez thanked them again and they expressed their gratitude for his presence at the canyon when they needed him. Hans especially hugged him like a brother.

"You and Juanita are always welcome at our farm in Sedona." Hernandez knew that Hans Snebly was a man of his word. He helped his wife onto her horse and waved goodbye.

Isabell prepared to bid them farewell, too. A sudden loneliness saddened her heart. Hans watched her. He had liked her from the very first moment he had met her, even under such tragic circumstances. Hans Snebly cleared his throat for the bluntest speech he had ever made in his life.

"Isabell, I don't know how deeply you are settled in this place, and I know you have your own house here, but if you want, you can come with me. I'm not rich, but we have a lovely farm. I have an awesome brother, and his family would surely welcome you. Leave all this behind, and come with me, please. I will never hurt you. I promise!"

Isabell looked at her house. She knew that if the body of John Harker was found in there, she would probably be accused of having killed her fiancé. Her parents were dead. Isabell Carson had no other family. She looked into Hans' eyes who gazed back with a hope and a warmth she had never seen in John's eyes. Hans reminded her of a cute puppy. Isabell smiled back at him and slowly nodded. "Yes, I will come with you, Hans Snebly. I have nothing to lose but a lot to gain, right?"

He hugged her carefully, then released her and looked at the others. "Armando, would you have my back one more time? There is something I have to do. He pulled his bandana over his mouth and entered Isabell's house while she stayed out. The stink of the decaying body made him gag as he closed the front door behind him. Inside Hans lit a lantern and smashed it on the ground. The room and the curtains immediately caught fire, and the flames leaped hungrily toward the corpse of John Harker on the ground. On his way out, Hans quickly grabbed a picture of a couple in a beautiful silver frame.

Snebly assumed it showed Isabell's parents and saved it from the flames. When he ran out of the house closing the door, he waved at Armando on the other side of the street. Immediately his Spanish friend yelled, "Fire, there is a fire!"

The townspeople ran toward the house, but it was a burning inferno so no one tried to put out the flames.

And none of the townsfolk paid attention to the group of four men and three women riding out of town with an unconscious outlaw thrown over the back of one of their horses. Meanwhile, another scum sat in the law dog's calaboose rubbing his swollen temple where the rock had hit him hard.

CHAPTER THIRTY-THREE

***

IT WAS TIME TO SAY GOODBYE TO HANS, NAICHE, AND ISABELL. BUT THEY KNEW they would see each other again in a few months. Elli's gratitude toward them was unlimited. Especially Naiche and his tribe held a special place in her heart. The Apache who had found her at the Nichol's ranch would always be family to her. She had saved him, and he had paid back the same favor by saving her life.

When Elli looked at Hans and Isabell, she knew they would be happy together. Isabell held the picture of her parents in her arms. Elli promised to visit them soon. "Please give my love to Anne and her husband William as well and thank Anne for the cross. Tell her it protected me well when you return it to her, my dear friend! I shall see you soon again. May God always be with you!"

Armando and Elli watched the others ride north. Then they turned their horses and continued toward Yuma along with their prisoner. Texas Logan faced a fair trial, and he was sentenced to death. He cursed the dead Sheriff Townsend and his beautiful daughter who stood below the gallows.

Armando had an arm around her shoulders while they watched the newly-appointed sheriff placing the hangman's noose around Texas Logan's neck.

"Are you ready for this?" Armando asked her gently. She looked at him, then back to the three-legged mare.

"Yes, sir. May God show his soul some mercy and my soul, too," she whispered.

Armando held her closer as they waited while the judge of the Territory read the sentence once again to Texas Logan and the townsfolk standing nearby. "Texas Logan, the entire town of Yuma know you murdered our sheriff as well as his deputy along with two other men who escorted the army transport. You have also been found guilty of murdering Jerome's bank clerk and six soldiers with the help of your pack of outlaws. You tried to kill the sheriff's daughter. Now you are sentenced to hang by the neck until you are dead, dead, dead. Do you have anything to say?"

Texas Logan stared down at Elli with a cold smile. "I'll see you in hell, little filly." When the priest began a prayer, Logan turned around and hissed at him "Take your Bible and prayer and get out of my face, sin-buster."

Elli gave a nod to the new sheriff, and the trapdoor under Texas Logan's boots opened with a creaking sound. He jerked and twisted. His neck didn't break, and it took him endless minutes to choke to death.

Finally, his legs stopped moving and he dangled in the afternoon breeze. It was over.

"How do you feel, Elli?" Armando looked into her eyes.

"Content and free, Armando. I kept my promise to my father, and I hope he can rest in peace now."

As she said it, she looked over to the town's small cemetery. Suddenly right there by the old oak with its huge branches she saw her father smiling at her, his sheriff's badge glistening in the sunshine. She tugged at Armando's sleeve and pointed toward the tree.

Her friend looked at the spot wondering what she wanted to show him, but her father had disappeared, carried away by the very gentle breeze that left an outlaw swinging on the rope of justice a few yards from the cemetery.

RECOGNITIONS FROM THE AUTHOR

* * *

THE CHARACTERS:

With the deepest respect for their history and culture, I acknowledge the following Apaches whose names I used for characters in this book. The stories of their lives have inspired me.

Kaywaykla: He was born as James Kaywaykla in 1876. His aunt was the famous female warrior Lozen who rode with Geronimo. James Kaywaykla was known to have been the last surviving warrior of Cochise's tribe. He helped to identify many photos of the past and died at age 83.

Dah Des Te: She was born around 1830. She was a female messenger and spy for Chief Geronimo. She married a second time after divorcing her first husband. The breakup of marriages wasn't uncommon among Native Americans.

She was said to have been able to shoot and ride like the best male warriors and helped negotiate the surrender of Geronimo. Dah Des Te was deported to Florida with the warriors who had surrendered. She was a close friend to Lozen, the most famous female warrior of the Apaches.

Naiche: He was the second son of Chief Cochise and a close friend of Geronimo.

He was a member of the Chiricahua Apaches (not Tonto as mentioned in this book). Naiche survived being imprisoned in Florida and Fort Sill in Oklahoma. He was one of the few who was allowed to move back to the Southwest and died in 1899 at age 55 on the Mescalero reservation in New Mexico.

Usen: This is the name used by the Apaches for their Creator God. He is said to live on top of a mountain in Arizona and that he created the earth with all of its plants, animals, and human beings.

Oscar Frank Townsend really was one of the sheriffs in Yuma, Arizona. He was appointed in 1871, but very little is known about his career as a lawman.

The name Werdinger I used for the character of the corrupt judge in Orange Grove is actually the name of a lawman as well. He lived in Yuma, Arizona. He was appointed as sheriff on September 26, 1864, and replaced the former lawman who had resigned. In April 1875, he was appointed as superintendent of the famous Yuma territorial prison. In 1877 he served a second term as sheriff of Yuma. Unlike my character in the book, he was known as a decent lawman.

Historical facts used in this book:

An archeological employee of the University of Arizona translated old Spanish documents. In some of them he found the astonishing story of an Irish immigrant who had been adopted by the Spanish King and gifted with a grant expanse of land in southern Arizona. It is documented that this man was respected as a white chief among some Native Americans of the area and that a mission with imported bells from Europe had been built on his estate.

The hacienda had been burned down by Apaches around 1780 according to the documents. The gold figures are indeed mentioned in those old papers, but neither the figures nor remains of the hacienda have ever been found.

The settlement of Sedona was indeed founded in 1899 by the Snebly family who originally came from Switzerland. Since all suggested village names were too long to receive permission for its own post office, the family finally suggested Snebly's wife's name, "Sedona", and the town carries the name to this day. Sedona has become world famous for its outstanding beauty as it is nestled into the red rock canyons. It is one of the most beautiful towns in Arizona.

The town of Castle Dome is a ghost town museum nowadays. It is about 35 miles from Yuma. Castle Dome was mainly famous for its lead mines, but even gold and silver were found there.

The town of Yuma is close to the Mexican border in Arizona. The main tourist attraction is the Territorial prison and the attached museum. The cell block was "part-time accommodation" for many outlaws, male and female. Even famous characters such as Buckskin Frank Lesley were imprisoned there.

A LOOK AT: A PROSPECTOR´S DREAM

***

The silver strike lures Kansas farmer Jesse Connor to Tombstone, Arizona.

Planning for a better life with his wife he faces unexpected betrayal and raging hate. What started as a vision for a better tomorrow soon turns into intrigue and attempted murder. Will his only true friends, an old miner and the most desired of shady ladies rescue him, or is the entrance to the mines of Tombstone the road to hell? Will he find unlimited wealth or will he lose everything, paying the ultimate price in the merciless Arizona territory?

AVAILABLE MARCH 2021

ABOUT THE AUTHOR

* * *

AS SOMEONE BORN AND RAISED IN GERMANY, AUTHOR MANUELA SCHNEIDER'S LOVE OF American Native and Western history might be surprising to some. But her fascination with pioneer life, cowboy heroes, and treacherous outlaws have been her constant companion for as long as she can remember.

As a child, Schneider recalls being mesmerized by American TV shows like Gun Smoke, Little House on the Prairie and Bonanza. In her adult years, Schneider fueled her deep interest in the American West by traveling to the U.S.A. and visiting historic sites like Tombstone, Monument Valley, and Kanab, UT. After experiencing the wild beauty of the Southwest first hand, her desire to write stories of love, struggle, and survival in the Wild, Wild West became even stronger.

After leaving a successful career designing motorcycle fashion for the European market, Schneider penned her first Western fiction novel in 2017.

When not researching or penning riveting stories about Western boomtowns and Native American life, Schneider can be found traveling all over the world, enjoying silver jewelry and spur smithing, studying archaeology as a hobby, and writing her own Western travel blog on manuelaschneider.com.